"I'm deeply concerned about our daughter."

John's face was somber. "In view of my financial standing, we can't rule out the possibility of her being kidnapped again, unless we take suitable precautions."

Hester eyed him suspiciously. "No doubt you have some plan ready. What do you propose?"

"Propose is exactly the word." His voice was deliberately matter-of-fact. "I provide you and Jo with a home, which is all I ask in return. I want to watch my daughter growing up, instead of having to snatch small doses of her company. And perhaps you and I could learn to live together. No demands on my part. I've got no wish to disrupt your life, Hester."

No wish to disrupt her life! John Ransome had done nothing else from the disastrous moment of their meeting.

CATHERINE GEORGE

innocent pawn

Harlequin Books

TORONTO • NEW YORK • LONDON
AMSTERDAM • PARIS • SYDNEY • HAMBURG
STOCKHOLM • ATHENS • TOKYO • MILAN

Harlequin Presents first edition February 1986
ISBN 0-373-10858-3

Original hardcover edition published in 1985
by Mills & Boon Limited

Printed in U.S.A.

CHAPTER ONE

HESTER paid off the taxi and ran up the garden path, eager to be home. She let herself into the house, her face bright with anticipation, calling 'Mother? Jo?' No answer. She dumped down her suitcase in the hall and frowning, shrugged off her raincoat. The house was very quiet. Unnaturally so. Puzzled, Hester took a quick look in the sitting-room then went along the hall to the big kitchen at the back of the house, half expecting to be jumped on playfully as she went, but the rooms were deserted, even the television blank. Beginning to feel uneasy Hester ran upstairs, deeply relieved to find her mother fast asleep on her bed. Smiling, she backed from the room. Chasing after a lively five-year-old for a few days was a full-time job, and entitled her mother to a nap, but Hester was surprised Jo had been put to bed early tonight. Certain her little daughter would be still wide awake just the same, Hester went along the landing to the door marked 'Jo's Room', and popped her head round it, a happy smile on her face. She stopped dead in the doorway, the smile frozen. The room was pin-neat; the bed empty.

Something was horribly wrong. Hester flew back to her mother and shook her awake urgently. Alicia Price woke with a start and sat up, blinking.

'Sorry, darling—must have dozed off. Good trip? Where's Jo?'

The blood drained from Hester's narrow face. 'What do you mean? Mother—isn't she here?'

Alicia scrambled off the bed, her eyes wide with consternation. 'But I understood you were collecting her from school, Hester—taking her out to tea.'

Hester's heart began thudding against her ribs. She swallowed hard and shook her head, her eyes bright with fear. 'I've only just arrived from Bath.'

They stared at each other in growing dread.

'They rang me from the school.' Alicia gripped her hands together, the lines deepening visibly in her face. 'They told me you'd collected Jo and asked them to pass on the message.'

Hester kept calm with effort, and touched her mother's hand gently.

'Who exactly were "they", Mother?'

Alicia gazed at her, stricken. 'Why, I—I don't know. The young woman who spoke to me just said "Highcroft School".' Her lips trembled. 'Hester—what have I done?'

'Now don't get upset, love.' Hester put a reassuring arm round her mother's shoulders. 'There must be a perfectly logical explanation.' She pushed a hand through her hair and tried to think rationally. 'It couldn't have been Miss Collins, her teacher. She sees me every day. It's most unlikely she'd hand my child over to someone else.' She glanced at her watch. 'After seven—the school will be closed for the weekend.'

'How about the headmistress's private number?' suggested Alicia, and pulled herself together resolutely. 'I'll put the kettle on while you look for it.'

Hester ran downstairs to the study and rummaged frantically through her battered filing cabinet for the file on Jo's school. She found Miss Beauchamp's private number on the Highcroft headed paper and dialled with unsteady fingers. The headmistress's crisp voice answered almost at once. After hearing Hester out she expressed deep concern. Josephine had been collected by her father during the lunch hour, an arrangement which she naturally thought was known to Hester. She disclaimed any knowledge of a message to Mrs Price, however, except that it could not have come from Miss Collins, as the young teacher was away from school with influenza. Hester apologised for troubling Miss Beauchamp, and put the 'phone down, her eyes like discs of green ice.

'What did she say?' Alicia put a mug of strong hot coffee in her hand.

'It appears that Jo's father has caused us all this anguish—not to mention exceeding his legal access.' Hester swallowed some coffee, her face stormy. 'No doubt he can provide some explanation, but my God, it had better be good!'

'Now Hester——' began Alicia, but her daughter waved her to silence.

'Please, Mother. Leave this to me.' Hester's jaw set ominously as she began to dial again, and with a worried frown Alicia went back to the kitchen.

Hester waited in a fury of impatience as the number rang repeatedly. He was certain to be at his desk, even at this hour, unless he was away. Not that he could be away. He had Jo. In which case, it occurred to her, he might not be in his palatial penthouse office either, unless Jo were with him. She stiffened when, at long last, the distinctive voice finally answered.

'This is Hester,' she said curtly, not bothering with a greeting. 'Just what have you done with my daughter?'

There was dead silence on the line for an instant before John Lauder Ransome answered distantly. 'Good evening, Hester. Perhaps you could be more precise. What exactly am I supposed to have done with *our* daughter? I haven't seen Jo since the twenty-seventh, which, in case it's slipped your mind, was the usual alternate Saturday you permit me to enjoy with her.' Suddenly his voice altered, roughening with urgency. 'What's wrong? What's happened, Hester?'

Hester's fingers tightened on the receiver.

'You mean Jo's not with you?'

'No, she is not! For God's sake explain.'

'I've been to Bath on a four-day course——' she began unsteadily.

'And it would have exceeded my legal rights to let me have Jo while you were away,' he said bitterly.

'It wasn't necessary. My mother took care of Jo, naturally.'

The deep breath he took was audible down the line. 'Go on, Hester,' he said heavily.

She repeated Miss Beauchamp's story, emphasising the fact that as far as the headmistress was concerned Jo's father had collected the child in the lunch-hour.

'The woman's talking rubbish,' said John Ransome brusquely. 'I know nothing about it.'

'Are you telling me the truth?' Hester's voice broke abruptly. '*Please*! Tell me if you've got Jo.'

'What kind of a monster do you think I am, Hester? Am I likely to lie about a thing like this? I wish to God I *could* say she was with me.' There was a pause. When he spoke again his voice was unemotional once more. 'Please try to keep calm, Hester. There's only one thing for it, I'm afraid. I must contact the police. Stay where you are—I'll be with you shortly.' He rang off without another word, and a sharp shudder of reaction ran through Hester as she leaned against the desk for a few moments after putting down the 'phone. Whereas before she had been merely furious at the thought of John whisking Jo off, now she was utterly shattered. Where in heaven's name *was* Jo? Wearily she went to join her mother in the kitchen. The hope in Alicia's eyes died a quick death at the sight of Hester's white, anguished face.

'She's not with John, then,' she said brokenly.

'No. He's calling in the police.' Hester rubbed a knuckle between her eyes. 'He—he obviously thinks Jo's been kidnapped. Neither of us was able to mention the possibility, let alone say the word.'

Alicia slumped down on one of the kitchen chairs.

'I feel so responsible.' She looked miserably at Hester. 'I should never have accepted the woman's word. How will I ever live with myself if—if——'

Hester reached out and squeezed her mother's hand hard.

'Put that thought out of your head right now, Mother. Of course you thought it was a bona fide message. Under the same circumstances I would have myself.'

Alicia straightened, taking in a deep breath.

'Thank you, darling. I'm sorry. Now. Have you eaten?'

'Not recently.' Hester drained the last of her coffee. 'But I don't want anything at the moment, thanks. I'll unpack my bag while—while we wait.'

There was a bad moment alone in her room when she unpacked the model Porsche she'd bought for Jo. An involuntary sob shook Hester's slender shoulders, but she stifled it at once, smiling damply at the thought of Jo's unfeminine preference for toys with wheels, even engines, rather than the usual dolls. Hester put the brightly-coloured box in the drawer of her bedside table and put her clothes away, then picked up Jo's photograph from the dressing table. The triumphant little face was a feminine version of her father's, except for the green eyes inherited from her mother. It was a school photograph, and Jo had been so proud of the brand new uniform, with its sober grey pinafore dress and absurd collar and tie. Hester's throat thickened. The knot of the tie was askew and the curly fair mop untidy, but the satisfaction in the dancing eyes was irresistible. Jo had been so proud of starting school. Hester brought herself up sharply. Jo still *was*. The present nightmare, all of it, was just some terrible mistake, and shortly the telephone or the doorbell would ring and someone would bring Jo back. Hester wished in vain she knew any of the other parents, but Jo had only been at the school a few weeks, and although she chattered constantly about the other children, it was only by their first names.

When the 'phone eventually did ring Hester raced down to the study and grabbed the instrument, almost dropping it in her frantic haste.

'Yes?' she said breathlessly.

'Mrs Ransome? Ione Beauchamp again. Is there news of Josephine? I really am most concerned.'

Hester's disappointment was so acute she felt physically sick.

'So am I,' she said. 'To be blunt, I'm frantic. Jo is not with her father, Miss Beauchamp. He knows nothing about her disappearance, and is just as—as worried as I am.'

'That's very disturbing news, Mrs Ransome. After your call earlier I made enquiries among my staff, and found that it was Mrs Page—the supply teacher deputising for Miss Collins—who was on duty in the playground at lunchtime. She handed Josephine over to a young man in chauffeur's uniform.'

'Go on,' prompted Hester urgently.

'That really is all I'm able to tell you. Normally no child is allowed to leave the premises unless collected by a parent, or at least a known representative. Mrs Page was unaware of the rule, therefore in this instance it was disregarded. I'm deeply sorry.'

'I see.' Hester felt winded. 'To be fair, Miss Beauchamp, I suppose Jo would have considered it quite normal to be collected by a chauffeur. As you know, my husband and I are divorced, and when Jo is picked up for her fortnightly outing with her father he sends a chauffeur to the house to avoid—disturbing me.' Which was one way of putting it, thought Hester wryly.

'I see. I, er, hesitate to bring the matter up,' went on the other woman delicately., but have you reported the occurrence to the police?'

'Jo's father is doing that. I expect to hear from them shortly.'

'Then may I make a request, Mrs Ransome? I know it must sound very materialistic and unfeeling in the circumstances, but could you give them my home address rather than the school should they wish to speak to me? I am only too anxious to help in any way I can, of course, but feel sure you understand that many of the children at my school are from titled and important families. Adverse publicity could be quite disastrous.'

'Oh yes, I understand,' answered Hester wearily.

'Thank you so much. It *is* the weekend, fortunately.'

Fortunately! Hester closed her eyes in horror as she put down the receiver. How on earth was she to survive a weekend without knowing what had happened to her child? Alicia had been hovering in the doorway and at the look on Hester's face hurried to hold her close, saying nothing until Hester was sufficiently recovered to tell her what Miss Beauchamp had said.

'The thing is, Mother, Jo wouldn't have thought twice about a chauffeur picking her up from school. None of the children there would, if it comes to that. My old Mini-Traveller stands out like a sore thumb rubbing shoulders with the chauffeur-driven Rolls and Bentleys outside the school every day.' Hester rubbed her eyes, sighing. 'I suppose I'd better wash and spruce myself up a bit to face the police.'

'How about eating something first?' suggested Alicia.

Hester shook her head, managing a faint grin.

'I've lived and breathed food for the past few days, Mother. I'll be glad to give it a rest. How about a drink instead?'

'Won't it knock us flat?'

'Not a bit of it. Might even help a little. Make it doubles while you're at it!' Hester ran up to her room to change her neat, navy wool suit and medium-heeled pumps for tweed slacks and a green mohair sweater, pushing her cold feet into comfortable suede boots. Her face was colourless with strain as she brushed her curly fair hair and pulled it into a loose knot on top of her head, adding a touch of colour to her mouth, her lips

trembling so much it made the task difficult as she
stared into the mirror, her mind full of Jo. She was
consumed with a burning desire to be doing something.
Anything. A gnawing frustration galled her at her own
inactivity, and she ran back down to the kitchen to
listen to a newscast on the transistor. The news items
were depressing enough, admittedly, but made no
mention of a child found injured, or ill, or worse, and
dispiritedly Hester went to the living room to join her
mother in front of the television. Alicia passed her a
glass of sherry.

'I thought I might as well watch the local news
programme,' she said, 'just in case . . .'

Hester nodded.

'The same thing occurred to me. I've been listening to
the radio. Nothing.' She put down the glass untasted,
and began to wander restlessly round the room. 'I
thought the police would have been here by now.
Someone ought to be *doing* something.' Both of them
stiffened as the doorbell rang, and Hester flew to
answer it.

In her hurry she forgot the safety chain. The door
jerked open only a few inches. At first glance the
aperture seemed filled by the tall figure of John Lauder
Ransome. He stood tall and still, the dim porch light
picking up glints in his smooth, ash-blond hair and
throwing his angular face into shadow.

The narrow entrance hall to the house was little more
than a passageway, and had an inner door with stained
glass panels, a small square porch separating it from the
solid outer door. Life-long habit had made Hester close
the glass door behind her before opening the outer one
to the cold night air, and now she stood trapped in the
little prison she had made for herself, trying to parry
the almost physical blow John Ransome's appearance
dealt her. She had spent years teaching herself never to
think of his compelling face and graceful body, to
pretend he didn't exist, yet now the sight of him was a

jolt even more severe than the first time she had ever laid eyes on him, particularly as the intervening years had added a formidable authority to the potency of his attraction.

Hester could find nothing to say, and he made no move to break the silence. Her pallor deepened and her poise, already badly undermined by the events of the past few hours, deserted her completely. The words of greeting she tried to summon up died unsaid. Her mouth dry and her pulse beating erratically, she stared up into the heavy-lidded grey eyes of the man who had once, so briefly, been her husband, but who was now transformed into an aloof, assessing stranger whose eyes very deliberately travelled from her face to her feet and back again as he waited for her to speak.

'Good evening,' John Ransome said at last. 'You seem—disappointed. Were you expecting someone else?'

The sound of the all too familiar voice, with the distinctive catch in it, broke Hester's spell.

'In a way.' She undid the chain with unsteady fingers, avoiding his eyes. 'A miracle, I suppose. Not terribly realistic of me to hope it would be someone returning Jo. And,' she added, closing the door behind him, 'I've been expecting the police.'

John turned on her, barring her way in the small porch.

'You were always bad for my self esteem, Hester. I still come way down your list.' The wry twist of his mouth brought the colour back to Hester's face. She eyed the hall beyond the glass door, feeling hemmed in by his presence in the narrow space.

'I'm sorry,' she said stiffly. 'I must have seemed rude, but——'

'But since our communications are normally made through the medium of the solicitors,' he put in suavely, 'you no doubt find it difficult to talk to me in the actual flesh—or does the word offend you?'

Hester glared at him, a furious light in her eyes.

'I meant that under the circumstances I'm not quite as much in command of the social niceties as I might be. My child is missing, and I'm nearly out of my mind with worry.'

'Our child,' he corrected swiftly, and took her arm as she tried to brush past him. 'Are you alone, Hester?'

'No. Mother's with me, as usual.' She pulled her arm away, dismayed to find she reacted strongly to his touch. His face hardened and he stepped back, as far away from her as the narrow space would allow.

'Do you really want her in on all this?' he asked shortly.

'Yes, of course. Why not?'

'I thought having the police here might distress her.' Hester's breath caught.

'Why?' Her eyes met his urgently. 'Are—are you trying to break something to me?'

'No. Nothing like that,' he said in swift reassurance, 'but sometimes their questioning must, of necessity, be to the point, and apart from her own information I thought you might want to shield her from the rest, for her own sake.'

'Mother would prefer it to being kept in the dark!' Hester fought to keep the sharpness from her tone and failed. He obviously thought very little about her own sensitivities, and it needled her. In actual fact all her nerve ends were raw and exposed. They literally quivered under the scrutiny of this man who was her husband and yet not her husband, who was so disturbingly familiar and yet so very much a stranger. His eyes looked tired and strained, but their clear clinical grey was the same as she remembered; colder perhaps, but just as searching. There were lines in his long, sharply sculpted face, particularly from the imperious nose to the corners of his wide, well-cut mouth, and some new, silvery streaks were added to the fairness of his thick, waving hair. He was dressed, as she always thought of him, in a soberly expensive grey suit, his shirt crisp and immaculate, the subtle silk tie precisely knotted, his shoes certain to be hand-made. In his presence Hester felt gauche and ill-groomed, and resented it. The silence grew.

'You've let your hair grow long,' he said at last.

Hester looked at him in surprise, and brushed past him. 'It saves time—and money.' She led the way to the living room and opened the door on a brass band concert broadcast at rather unaccustomed volume. 'Mother's in here.'

Alicia got up and switched off the television, smiling in welcome.

'Hello, John.' She held out her hand.

An answering smile lit his eyes for the first time as he took her hand in his.

'How are you, Alicia?'

'Not at my best, I'm afraid. I feel so guilty——'

'Mother, don't,' implored Hester. 'You mustn't blame yourself. It wasn't your fault.'

'She's right, Alicia,' said John reassuringly, patting her hand. He looked across at Hester. 'I gave the police the details; and in their opinion this was all carefully planned. Whoever has Jo obviously knew your movements.'

'Then they do think she's been kidnapped.' Hester's legs suddenly gave up on her, and she slumped on a low stool near the fireplace. His face sombre, John motioned Alicia to the sofa, and seated himself beside her.

'Once they knew who I was they assumed it was certain. Harrison, my assistant, is at the house at this moment on standby, someone else at the office, both waiting to hear from whoever has Jo. If you should be contacted here, Hester, get in touch with me at once.'

Alicia made a small sound of distress, and Hester

shot a hostile look at John.

'Your money is the cause of all this.'

'No doubt it is.' His eyes were bleak as he turned away, ostensibly to look round the room. 'Nothing has changed, I see.'

'No, nothing,' said Hester briskly. 'It suits us very well. The house may be a little small by some standards, but for us the great advantage is the size of the kitchen—very necessary in my line of work.'

'Any line of work is totally *un*necessary as far as you're concerned.' John retorted instantly. 'The allowance I make you is more than adequate for both you and Jo to live on in comfort.'

'I prefer to support myself,' said Hester tartly. 'I don't need your money. It's all invested for Jo's future.'

'You have no necessity at all to provide for her future!'

'I disagree.'

There was a nasty silence as green eyes clashed with grey, and Alicia got up hurriedly, plainly bent on escape.

'May I offer you a drink, or coffee, John? Have you had anything to eat?' she asked, making for the door.

He sprang to his feet, the ice in his eyes melting as he smiled at her. 'I'm not hungry, thanks, Alicia, but coffee would be marvellous.'

The door closed behind her small, slim figure, leaving Hester flushed bright red with mortification, bitterly conscious of her lack of hospitality.

'I apologise.' She had to force the words out. 'I should have offered you something before, but I—but——' Her voice failed, and a great sob tore through her. She hid her face in her hands and fought to hold back the tears welling through her fingers. John watched her in silence for a moment then pulled her to her feet, holding her against him. Hester stiffened, then relaxed, turning her head wearily into his shoulder. 'Oh Jack,' she whispered, 'I'm going out of my mind. She's so small. I know she's plucky and independent, but she must be terrified.' The darker, unspoken fears she left buried in the back of her mind, too horrific even to put into words.

John's arms tightened round her, his voice unrecognisable as he said 'I'll get her back. I promise you. If it means handing over every last penny I can raise.' His eyes were hard as he turned up her face to meet his. 'I mean it. Jo is as much my child as she is yours, Hester. And I love her just as much as you do—more, perhaps, since it all has to be compressed into the miserly ration of her company you allow me.'

Hester pulled away at once, the fleeting moment of closeness vanished.

'I keep to the letter of the agreement,' she said flatly.

'Oh yes,' said John bitterly. 'With no leeway in any direction. You know perfectly well I have no choice but to be away on the stipulated dates on occasion, but do you ever allow me some other day in lieu, Hester? Well? Do you?'

She sat down again, her face averted.

'We have an agreement. I see no point in altering it as and when it suits *you*.'

'No. I'm very much aware of that. You still take infinite pleasure in making me pay.'

Her head flew up, her eyes hot as they saw the sardonic expression in his. 'That's not true. Besides, Jo is far more my daughter than she is yours.'

'Only because you insist on it being that way,' he retorted. There was a charged silence, while each of them tried for calm. 'Your mother is being very tactful,' he said at last, 'leaving us alone.'

Hester nodded.

'Poor dear—she feels wretched because it happened while I was away.'

'And that's why it did happen. Because you were away.' His voice cut like a whiplash. 'If you had been where you should have been, or even let me have Jo while you were away, none of this would have happened.'

Hester went white with outrage. She glared at him, her breasts rising and falling rapidly in her agitation. John's eyes were drawn like a magnet to the curves outlined by the soft wool of her sweater, and the colour rushed back to her cheeks, then receded again.

'You cold, unfeeling swine,' she bit out, and hunched over, her arms hugged across her chest. 'How can you be so grossly callous at a time like this? Can't you understand what I'm going through? My child has been taken from me——'

Too late she realised her mistake. As soon as the words were out Hester could have bitten her unruly tongue. She knew only too well what was coming as John sat down again on the sofa. He leaned back, one long leg crossed casually over the other, and smiled at her pleasantly.

'Who better, Hester? *You* took my child away from *me* almost as soon as she was born, in that very expensive private room whose fees I paid,' he added.

'Money!' She looked at him with dislike. 'That's the only thing you understand. It's surprising you never proposed *buying* Jo from me.'

'I would have—if I'd have thought there was the remotest chance of success.' He raised an eyebrow and took a cigar case from his pocket. 'Do you mind?'

Hester bit back her answer as her mother appeared with a tray. John sprang to take it from her, chatting to Alicia easily as he set it down where she instructed, then allowing himself to be plied with smoked salmon sandwiches. Not the best of choices, thought Hester acidly, fancying John's eyebrows rose a trifle at the expensive delicacy.

'We don't always eat so extravagantly,' she felt obliged to point out. 'You're actually finishing up leftovers from one of my recipes.'

'I thought you specialised in puddings and desserts

these days,' he said casually.

Hester shot a surprised look at him. 'How did you know that?'

'I follow your career with interest.' He turned to accept a cup of coffee from Alicia with a smile.

'You mean you keep tabs on me,' said Hester acidly. 'Making sure Jo is brought up in suitably proper manner!'

The look he turned on her was arctic. 'I obviously failed there, or this would never have happened.'

His words struck Hester like a body blow. 'That's unfair! Jo was kidnapped because of your money, not my lack of care.' She wiped away sudden tears with ferocity, and turned her back on him rudely. Whatever response John Ransome might have made was interrupted by the doorbell. Hester shot to her feet, tears drying on her cheeks, her eyes blazing with hope, but John laid a restraining hand on her arm.

'It's probably the police. I'll answer it.'

Hester huddled close to Alicia on the settee as he left the room. Neither of them said a word as the murmur of masculine voices sounded in the hall before John ushered in two men.

'Hester, this is Detective Inspector Mason and Detective Sergeant Denney. My wife, gentlemen, and Mrs Price, my mother-in-law.'

'Good evening.' The inspector was a dark, alert-eyed man in his early forties. He waved his fair, large sergeant to a chair near the door to take notes, then sat near Hester at her invitation. John balanced on the arm of the sofa, his own arm along the back behind Hester, while the inspector questioned both women on every last scrap of information that could possibly be of help in recovering Jo. Almost as an afterthought Inspector Mason asked Hester gently.

'And you have no idea who might have taken your daughter?'

'Of course not. If I did I'd be hounding them right

now, Inspector, using force, if necessary, to get her back,' said Hester scornfully, then started as John laid a hand on her shoulder. She shook it off impatiently, and cried, 'Why are we just sitting here *talking* about it? Why isn't someone *doing* something?'

'I appreciate the way you feel, Mrs Ransome,' said Inspector Mason, 'but without the necessary facts our task will be twice as difficult.'

Hester subsided, a little ashamed of her outburst.

'I'm sorry. What else would you like to know?'

'I'd like a list of your men-friends and their addresses, or any other associates you may have.' The policeman glanced up at John's stony face. 'I'm sure Mr Ransome would leave us alone for a moment if you prefer the information to remain confidential.'

'My—Mr Ransome has no need to leave us.' Hester's shoulders squared proudly. 'I see no man socially, and only a very few in the line of business. The latter include Monsieur Alain Girardin, the manager of the Imperial, some of the chefs there, my doctor . . . I can't think of anyone else, unless one includes the men who service my car and empty my dustbin.'

The inspector tactfully ignored her sarcasm. 'And what about women-friends?'

'An old friend, Lucy Miles, comes occasionally for a visit. She's a teacher in North London. There's the young catering student who helps me on weekends, Joanna Carter, and my mother has a friend, Mrs Drayton, who's in and out most days, but otherwise I don't really see anyone much. I don't get time for anything more demanding in the social line.'

'You never go out at all?' asked the inspector.

Hester smiled suddenly, an unexpected flash of amusement in her eyes, despite their swollen lids. She looked over her shoulder at John. 'I do go to the cinema, admittedly, but only to matinées to see things like *The Sound of Music* and *Jungle Book* with my little girl.'

John grinned back at her, his face lightening for a moment.

'Jo made me take her to that the other Saturday.'

'And I took her the week before—for the second time!'

They laughed a little, but only for a moment. Almost immediately the haunted look was back on Hester's face and she turned away, the moment losing out to the prevailing tension. Then something else occurred to her, and she hesitated.

'There is someone else I see, now I come to think of it.' Hester kept her face firmly averted from John. 'It hardly seems relevant, though.' Even without looking at him she could sense that John had stiffened.

'Any detail you can furnish may be of use,' the inspector assured her.

'My daughter and I visit Mrs Michael Desmond occasionally, and she sometimes visits us here,' said Hester rapidly, aware in every fibre of John's displeasure.

'And who is Mrs Desmond?' asked Inspector Mason, his eyes intent.

'My sister,' said John without inflection. 'She lives near Burford.'

'As you say,' agreed the inspector, looking from one to the other, 'it hardly seems relevant in this instance. Or have you met other people at Mrs Desmond's house, Mrs Ransome?'

'Not—not since Jo was born.' Painful colour rose in Hester's cheeks and she was deeply thankful John had chosen to sit where he had. For the moment she had no wish to meet his eyes, much less to see his anger. To learn of her visits to Camilla in the presence of the police was hardly likely to endear her to him. As John rose to see the two men out she looked at him warily, but his face gave nothing away. As he left the room only the rigidity of his shoulders gave any sign that John Lauder Ransome was in a towering rage.

CHAPTER TWO

THE house was very quiet after the police left. Hester felt uneasy as she gathered up coffee cups and neglected sandwiches, and any hopes of escaping to the kitchen were dashed when John told her curtly to come straight back after leaving the tray with Alicia. He held the door open for her, looking down at her inscrutably.

'I think we should have a talk, Hester; all about the esoteric delights of these sojourns in Burford.'

Alicia was only too glad to leave them to it. She retired to her bedroom, preferring to watch her portable television alone than remain with John and Hester, the atmosphere they were creating between them too abrasive for her much-tried nerves.

When Hester went reluctantly back to the living-room John was standing by the fireplace, staring down at the imitation logs of the gas fire.

'Why don't you have that cigar now?' she suggested, hoping to inject a degree of warmth into the cold cross-currents eddying between them. He turned absently, shaking his head.

'No, thanks. Do you have any whisky? Perhaps we could both have a drink.'

This seemed an even better idea, and Hester went back to the kitchen with alacrity, taking her time before returning with a bottle of scotch, a jug of water, a decanter of sherry and some glasses. She put the tray down on a small table, poured herself a modest quantity of sherry and motioned John to help himself. In silence she sat down on one of the winged arm chairs while he poured half a tumbler of spirit and topped up the glass with water before seating himself opposite her in a wry travesty of domesticity.

'Do you think the police will really be able to do anything, Jack?' she asked.

'They'll do all the routine things thoroughly, make extensive enquiries and so on, but if she has been kidnapped——' John swallowed half the whisky before going on. 'Until I get a demand for money, frankly I don't see what anyone can do.' He stared broodingly into his glass, his brows drawn together.

'But don't—don't kidnappers tell one not to inform the police?' asked Hester unsteadily. 'Or do I watch too much television?'

'I can't understand why they're so slow off the mark,' he answered musingly. 'They might know I'd have contacted the police by now. I would have expected some sort of communication before this.' His eyes softened as they rested on her face. 'Try not to upset yourself too much, Hester. When I *am* contacted you can be sure I'll do exactly as I'm asked—anything in the world to get Jo back, I promise.'

Hester felt all at sea. It was evident John really adored the child, whereas all along Hester had taken his insistence on access to their daughter as sheer bloody-mindedness rather than a real desire to spend time with the child. It seemed she was mistaken. She looked at him reflectively. He was very attractive, despite the remote, withdrawn expression his face had taken on since their last meeting. Contained, decided Hester. That was the word for him these days. The John Ransome of five years ago had been more extrovert. She flushed as she realised he was staring back.

'That's a very dissecting sort of expression in your eyes,' he said. 'I feel rather like a specimen under a microscope.'

'I—I was just thinking how much Jo resembles you.' A hasty improvisation, but true enough.

'Not entirely. She has your eyes, Hester.' John turned away and finished the last of his drink. 'You must let me know the moment anyone contacts you. Time could be of maximum importance if they get in touch with you first.'

'Yes, of course.' She drew in a shaky breath. 'Where—I mean will you be at home tomorrow?'

'I was due in Paris tonight for the weekend, but I've cancelled, of course.'

Some dishy lady must be disappointed, thought Hester cattily, then paid attention hastily as she realised John was repeating some instructions, an impatient frown on his face.

'Please listen carefully, Hester,' he said coldly. 'I said I'll keep in touch with you during the day, but if you want me in a hurry you have a choice of three numbers, office, home or car. I'll brief my people in advance.' His fingers touched hers as he handed her a card. 'I'll move heaven and earth, Hester.'

'Yes. I know you will.' Hester withdrew her hand quickly and stood up to take his glass. 'A refill?'

'I shouldn't, but God knows I need one. Thank you. Where's Alicia?'

'Lying on her bed, worrying herself to shreds.'

'Wouldn't she be better here with us than by herself?'

'I suggested it, but Mother apparently finds the company of her television rather more restful than ours.'

John regarded her in silence for a moment, then said casually, 'Then let's talk about you and Camilla, shall we?'

Hester's mouth compressed.

'I thought you might have let the matter drop under the circumstances.'

John smiled mockingly.

'From your own past experience of my tenacity you should know me better than that.'

The sardonic note in his voice flicked Hester on the raw.

'How true,' she said sweetly. 'But it's not as if I've committed a crime.'

John tapped a fingernail against his glass consideringly, as if passing judgment.

'Not so much a crime I suppose, as a sin. One of omission, as the church puts it, rather than *com*mission.'

'You can hardly expect me to agree,' she said resentfully, 'and at this time of night, and under these particular circumstances, the last thing I need is a sermon.'

His face darkened, and he looked away.

'No. I apologise.'

This time the silence was longer, and even more uncomfortable until Hester said quietly, 'Camilla, at least, will be glad you know I visit her. She always wanted to tell you, but I wouldn't let her.'

'Why, for God's sake?' he demanded with violence. 'Did you expect me to come storming into my sister's house and wrest our child from your arms?'

'No. Our acquaintance was short, admittedly, but during its entire duration I knew of only one unpremeditated action of yours as far as I was concerned.' Hester turned a steady green gaze on John's hostile face. He winced slightly, but had himself in hand again, almost at once, the usual guard firmly back in place.

'Since then, my dear Hester, it's been a trifle difficult to act on impulse when communicating through solicitors!'

She flushed, and ignored his thrust.

'Camilla gets lonely with Mike away so much,' she went on. 'She loves to see Jo——'

'And I do not? I, of course, am merely a father as opposed to an aunt, but even so can be forgiven for wondering why Camilla should be so much more fortunate than I am in this respect!' John got to his feet and stood looking down his nose at Hester, his eyes cold.

'Because she likes to see *me*, too. That's the

difference.' Hester returned his look, undismayed. 'We just chat together over tea, and Jo plays with the animals. Nothing underhand about any of it. Except that I made Camilla promise not to mention it to you in case——'

'In case I put a stop to it, Hester? My God, is that how you see me? As a killjoy who can't bear to let his child enjoy herself with someone else?'

'No, of course not, Jack. Stop putting words in my mouth. I—I merely assumed you wouldn't approve of Camilla associating with me, that's all.'

John shook his head in sarcastic wonder.

'Did you really!'

'Yes, I did. Anyway, it's only a couple of months since we came across each other again. She and Mike went off to live in Holland soon after you and I were divorced, as you know, so apart from Christmas cards and the odd letter I hadn't been in touch with Camilla for years until I bumped into her in the foodhall at Astley's. We had tea together, and something of a heart to heart.' Hester turned away, hesitating.

'And?' prompted John.

'Well—apparently Camilla's been suffering from this guilt complex about us.'

'She has no reason to. None of it was her fault.'

'I told her the same thing, but she seems to think that as you and I first—encountered each other at her house she is somehow to blame. Which is illogical, I suppose, but women are, sometimes.' Hester stole a look at him, but glanced away hurriedly. There was something decidedly unnerving about John Ransome in his present frame of mind. 'You and I said some bitter things to each other,' she went on doggedly. 'The prospect of meeting you at Camilla's was embarrassing. I felt instinctively that after the divorce you would want none of your family to have anything to do with me.'

'But then, your instincts are seldom accurate, Hester, unless you've changed out of all recognition.' John shrugged. 'Rest assured you and Cam may consort to your hearts' content without any interference from me. I've no objection—on any count. In fact, this all seems a trifle unimportant at the moment.'

Hester's shoulders drooped. She knew only too well what he meant. It seemed pointless to wrangle over minor issues when all the time their child was somewhere out there, missing, stolen like a piece of merchandise taken from a shop.

'Hester—don't look like that.' John held out a hand and she put hers into it, taking an unexpected comfort from his warm clasp. 'I must go, talk things over with Harrison and get things rolling if money is involved.'

'The root of all evil,' murmured Hester.

John dropped her hand and went to the door.

'The trick is, Hester, to look past the money to the man behind it.' He gave her a wintry smile. 'Try to sleep, and say goodnight to your mother for me. I'll ring you in the morning unless—well, don't hesitate to ring *me* if you need anything, anything at all. Goodnight.'

'Goodnight,' she answered forlornly, and sat staring at the door as it closed behind John's tall, elegant figure. She felt dazed, adrift, all her carefully maintained defences crumbled and disintegrating from the impact of seeing John face to face once more. She was appalled at her own involuntary reaction to meeting him again. Standing there in silence in her doorway he might have been some charismatic stranger rather than the man she had divorced. She was ashamed to acknowledge that the shock of his physical presence had almost blotted out the crisis which had made their confrontation necessary. Hester took herself in hand sharply. The entire situation was abnormal, she reminded herself. Her nerves were frayed with fear about Jo—was it any wonder her immunity to the famous Ransome charm was less tenable than usual. It was simply that she had none of her usual forces to marshal against him. At this her train of thought braked to a halt. If her immunity was really genuine, surely no forces should have been necessary. This unpalatable truth was the final straw. Hester began to shiver, and gripped her hands in her lap, clenching her jaws to stop her teeth chattering. The whole evening had been like a bad dream. Any moment now she would wake up to find herself with nothing more exacting on her mind than getting Jo to school and creating an endless supply of gateaux and soufflés to keep a roof over their heads. Only it was no dream, and Jo's bed was empty, and if she were totally honest there was no need to work to pay the rates. Suddenly everything was too much, and Hester sank to the floor, succumbing to a desolation too austere and bleak even for tears, curling herself into a foetal ball of despair that was oblivious even to her mother's hand on her shoulder until Alicia grew urgent, shaking her to life.

'Hester! Don't give in like that. What if Jo should walk in right now——'

Hester scrambled to her feet, ashamed. 'I'm sorry. It all piled up into one great load of misery for a moment.' She took a deep breath and squared her shoulders. 'I won't let it happen again, I promise. Let's go and eat something.'

In spite of her brave words it was hard for Hester to force down the scrambled eggs they chose for a snack. She was secretly very concerned about Alicia, who looked haggard and drawn, and persuaded her to take a sleeping pill to help her to rest. When Hester was satisfied her mother was settled down in bed, looking reasonably drowsy, she had a bath, then curled up in a corner of the sofa in the living room, unable to face the confines of her bedroom and the loneliness of the dark. It was easier to sit in the light, drinking coffee and leafing through cook books, keeping her vigil with as much fortitude as possible, even though nothing blotted out thoughts of Jo. Hester kept wondering if her child were sleeping, or hungry, or locked up somewhere alone, crying. She closed her mind violently against the last, springing up with a shiver to pace the room, her untidy curls growing steadily wilder as she raked a restless hand through them. She fretted the minutes away, waiting tensely for a 'phone call that never came, and aware that this was the road to hysteria Hester tried vainly to think of something, anything, to take her mind off the present agony. Eventually she sat down again, a bitter little smile on her face as she conceded that only one subject had the power to take her mind off Jo. The past.

Hester's meeting with John Lauder Ransome had come about as a direct result of the career she chose. At catering college she had teamed up with Lucy Miles, a dark, lively girl from London, and become firm friends; so much so they decided to set up in partnership together after qualifying. Between them they established a small business catering for buffet lunches and dinners, functioning from Hester's own home, where she and her mother had lived alone since the death of her father while she was still at school. Alicia Price had money of her own, enough to remain in the comfortable pre-war house near Oxford and send her daughter to college, even to put up some of the capital for the little business Hester and Lucy eventually embarked on with such enthusiasm.

They did remarkably well right from the start. Lucy was blessed with a keen business sense, which, allied to Hester's culinary flair, made their venture prosper quickly as a viable commercial concern. The Price household was fortunately possessed of a large kitchen, which Alicia modified and streamlined to the girls' requirements as they built up their reputation in an area which went in for supper parties and bridge teas in a big way, as well as cricket club dances and the usual wedding breakfasts. Hester got hold of a second-hand Mini-Traveller, and they delivered their delicacies to clients anywhere within a ten mile radius. Normally whichever girl was delivering deposited the ready-made dishes and departed, but occasionally a request was made for Hester or Lucy to stay to supervise the meal, usually when a more complicated dish needed reheating, or finishing touches at the last moment.

It was Hester's turn to do the necessary when Camilla Desmond contacted them to cater for a party to celebrate her tenth wedding anniversary. She called at the house in person, a tall, friendly young woman with fair hair and a prominent nose, who was frankly taken aback at the youth of the two caterers. Hester, in particular, looked very much younger than twenty-two, with her short mop of streaky blonde curls. Lucy, on the other hand, had smooth dark hair coiled high on her head, and an air of maturity which was useful in reassuring clients of the firm's competence. After only a few minutes chat Camilla and Hester got on together like a house on fire, the only snag the fact that the Desmonds' house was thirty miles or so away, well beyond the boundary line the girls had set themselves. Camilla got round this by insisting on paying extra for the petrol and inviting Hester to stay the night of the party and join in the fun herself. Hester was doubtful at first, but eventually gave in, the weather too cold and frosty for her to relish the prospect of driving over dark, icy roads for miles after putting on a three-course buffet supper for forty people. The guest-list was to be rather cosmopolitan, including some French business associates of the host and some people from the nearby American Airforce base as well as a sprinkling of the Desmonds' neighbours. Camilla's request was for something solidly British for the main course, with foreign variations for starters and dessert. The menu eventually devised was a Salade Nicoise, succulent with artichokes, olives and anchovies, followed by traditional steak and kidney pie, and rounded off with chocolate chiffon pie, English trifle and petits fours, plus a cheeseboard as international and varied as the two girls could make it.

Hester smiled wearily as she remembered how confident and enthusiastic she had been, setting off with her carload of goodies and her overnight bag. Her black crêpe dress had been the one kept for this type of evening, easily covered by a smock while she prepared the meal for the table, and smart enough for her to mingle with the guests afterwards. She had been jubilant over the success of the meal, and confident of netting more clients during the evening, which was the main reason for making the effort to join the party, despite the usual fatigue which set in once the meal had been served and cleared away. The Desmonds were very kind, introducing her to everyone and making sure she was well looked after, Camilla very disappointed about the non-appearance of her brother, who was apparently the boy wonder of electronics, at present on his way back from the States and due to turn up at the party. The subject was forgotten by Hester as a tall American officer asked her to dance, and the following hour passed so pleasantly it came as something of a surprise to realise she was actually very weary when there was a break in the music. Bed became imperative, and quite suddenly she was dead on her feet. Hester took leave of the friendly American, and after a word with Camilla went up to the guest room, which was situated at the back of the house, well away from the festivities.

Almost walking in her sleep Hester undressed and got into bed, hardly aware that the bedside lamp went out before she could switch it off. She turned to burrow contentedly into the pillows, asleep almost at once. At some time during the night she began to dream. A vivid real dream. Someone was touching her, familiar, beloved fingers were caressing her body and she was arching and stretching like an ecstatic kitten beneath the coaxing, stroking fingers, delight coursing through her veins. And then the dream became nightmare as she suffocated under a heavy weight in the blanketing dark, bound by cruel ropes that tied her down, and a gag that kept her from screaming. In her frantic struggles to be free she woke fully to find it was no dream, but the reality of a man's body on hers. The smell of whisky was strong in her nostrils, the man's arms like steel bands holding her while his mouth and tongue kept her from uttering anything more than a choked gurgling as she tried to scream in protest at what he eventually succeeded in doing no matter how fiercely he fought to prevent it. Then it was over and she was free as the man rolled away and flopped on his back beside her, heavily asleep the moment his head touched the pillow.

Shivering and sick with disgust, tears scalding her cheeks, Hester crawled out of bed and tried to switch on the lamp, but nothing happened. She wanted passionately to see her unwanted bedfellow in the light, to memorise his face, but in the end she gave up her search for another light switch, afraid of waking him. She groped for her little pile of clothes and her overnight bag, then crept silently along the hall to the bathroom she had used earlier, risking a chance encounter with anyone else. Locked inside she washed and dressed at top speed, avoiding her face in the mirror, feeling degraded and cheapened, but swallowing the sobs that shook her as she crept down the staircase and through the dark, deserted hall.

The car had sounded unnervingly loud as Hester started it up in the silent dark outside the house. The Desmonds lived on the outskirts of one of those timeless Cotswold villages ten miles from anywhere, and there was nothing on the road as she edged the car out of the drive. An hour later she was home, back in the restorative safety of the solid, respectable house in the tree-lined suburban road, its familiarity helping to re-establish the lost identity taken from her in the nightmarish experience of just a short time before.

Hester had drunk three cups of a brew strong enough to dissolve the spoon by the time her mother came down, all the time trying to think rationally and reasonably of what had happened and get it in perspective. If she were brutally frank with herself the experience had not been unmitigated nightmare, at least, not at first. She deliberately made herself relive those first few dreaming moments, going over them again and again. Her senses had responded to the unseen hands with an undeniable, joyous recognition which had transported her anonymous lover into a state of frenzy that shocked her dreaming delight into waking terror. Only 'lover' was hardly the word. Hester's mouth twisted as she thought of an alternative. 'Rapist' was too strong; inaccurate, too, to be fair, and 'ravisher' had an archane, creaking sound to it. 'Larcenist', perhaps. He—whoever he was—had undisputably stolen something of value from her, however intangible. Hester propped her head in her hands. staring dry-eyed into her coffee. She blamed herself bitterly. She should have fought like a wildcat from the start. But in the beginning she had thought she was dreaming, she argued with herself. Those subtle caresses had belonged to fantasy not to waking reality. Her body, never having experienced anything like them before, had responded before her mind was aware of any danger. Besides, it was no big thing. It happened all the time. To other people, admittedly, not to her, but nevertheless a commonplace occurrence. It was a pity the wait for someone special had been in vain, of course, for the incomparable lover of every girl's dreams she had imagined would introduce her to the so-called delights of love. Hester assured herself she would be able to laugh about the entire thing in time. The whole episode smacked of farce—wrong room, wrong bed, and the villain of the piece so inebriated he would never recognise her again if he met her in the street. That was the worst part. To be treated as a *thing*, a mere body in the dark. Hester shuddered.

* * *

It was late the same afternoon when Alicia came into the warm, cluttered kitchen, rather an odd expression on her face. Lucy and Hester were up to their elbows in quiches and vol-au-vents for a christening party, the latter too pre-occupied, one way and another, to notice as her mother looked at her questioningly and told her there was someone in the office asking for Miss Price. Hester went along the hall to what had once been the family dining room, and was now furnished with a large, workmanlike desk, a filing cabinet and had shelves filled with cookery books. She paused in the doorway, surprised to see a man standing at the window, his back towards her. Her clients were always women. This client was very definitely male, tall and slim, with thick, waving hair as fair as her own, his shoulders wide beneath a waxed Barbour shooting jacket. Suddenly conscious of her apron and untidy hair Hester coughed slightly and closed the door behind her. Her unknown visitor spun round and stood very still, staring at her in stunned surprise. Hester looked back uncertainly, prey to an uneasy feeling of recognition.

'Good afternoon,' she said. 'You asked for me?'

'Are *you* Miss Price?' The man was deathly pale, the marks very pronounced beneath his light grey eyes.

Ignoring her inner misgivings Hester waved him to a chair as she sat behind her desk, wondering apprehensively if he were ill.

'Yes. Won't you sit down?'

He shook his head and stayed where he was.

'I think it's best I stay on my feet. My name is John Lauder Ransome.'

'How do you do.' The name meant nothing to her. 'I'm Hester Price. How can I be of help to you?'

His long, rather imperious face went even paler.

'I don't think you can. I'm Camilla Desmond's brother. Does that give you an inkling of why I'm here?'

Hester sat very still, a haunted look dawning in her eyes as she stared up at him. 'You've come to settle Mrs Desmond's account?' she asked, without much hope.

'No. I think it's more to the point to settle my own.' His voice was very attractive, and had an odd, distinctive little catch in it.

Hester looked away, and clasped her hands together, noting absently that they were trembling. 'I don't understand you, Mr Ransome.'

He moved from the window and came to the desk, leaning on his hands as he bent towards her, his voice quiet and urgent.

'I woke this morning to an almighty crash, Miss Price. My sister dropped a tray of morning tea when she found me sleeping in the bed where she expected to find you.'

A great tide of heat rushed through Hester, and she kept her head down, refusing to look at him.

'So it was *you*,' she said, almost inaudibly. Nausea rose in her throat, and she swallowed convulsively. John Ransome took in a deep, shaky breath.

'What in God's name can I say, or do?'

Hester pushed back her chair and stood up, looking at him with a shiver of distaste. 'Nothing. Just go, Mr Ransome. I have work to do.'

'Please!' His eyes held hers in desperation. 'Let me explain. My flight from the States was delayed, and I arrived at Cam's just as the last guest was departing down the drive. Mike, my brother-in-law, stayed down and had another drink with me to celebrate the success I had with my trip to the States. Only it wasn't just one drink, unfortunately, and he forgot to tell me I was sleeping in a different room from my usual berth. By the time I went to bed I was suffering from too much alcohol on an empty stomach, coupled with jet-lag. The light didn't seem to be working in the guest room, so I just stripped off my clothes in the dark and fell into bed. I went to sleep immediately, but some time in the night I half woke to find a body against mine. I must have thought I was dreaming—I hardly remember— God, how else can one explain behaving like a sex-mad cretin?' He turned away in self-disgust. 'All I can say is that I was no way in control of my actions and my baser instincts ran riot. I assure you that force is not my style.'

Hester could well believe that. The situation was probably normally in reverse, with hordes of females pressing their attentions on the highly attractive Mr Ransome. Which fact did nothing at all to soften her attitude towards him.

John Ransome turned back to her, wincing a little at the ice-cold look in her eyes, but looking at her steadily.

'There is another factor driving me frantic, Miss Price. It may cause you distress, but I have to know— did I frighten you, hurt you in any way?'

'Of course I was frightened—clear out of my wits!' Hester ran a hand through her short curls, her face hostile. 'You may be accustomed to strangers in your bed in the night, Mr Ransome; I most definitely am not. The entire episode was a nightmare, and I just want to put it out of my mind.'

'Did I injure you?' he persisted.

'I do have some bruises, yes; rather inevitable under the circumstances. I thought it was a dream, too. When I woke up fully I put up a fair fight, but you were very intent on getting your own way whatever I did. And having got it you promptly passed out, sprawled on your back in an alcoholic stupor.' By this time Hester was literally shaking with disgust, and turned her head away in disdain, ignoring the look of sick distaste on John Ransome's good-looking face.

There was silence for a moment before he said slowly, 'I don't know how to make amends—what to say or what to do.' He looked at her averted profile, his jaw taut. 'There's no giving back what I took from you——'

'What?' She swung round in consternation. 'How did you—what do you mean?'

A dull flush spread over his face.

'I was left in no doubt,' he said with difficulty. 'Camilla—the sheets——'

Hester gave a frantic little moan and turned away, white to the lips.

'Please. Go away,' she got out. 'Now!'

John Ransome put a hand out towards her instinctively.

'Miss Price——'

'Before I scream the place down—get out of my sight!' Hester turned her back on him, her hands so tightly clenched her fingernails punctured the skin of her palms. He stood frowning in silence for a tense moment, his eyes sombre as they rested on the bowed, curly head. Then he went from the room, closing the door very quietly behind him. Hester heard her mother's voice in the hall, and John Ransome's voice replying, then the front door closed and she sagged, sitting down at her desk with a bump.

'Hester? What's the matter? Who was that?' Alicia Price put her arm round her daughter's trembling shoulders in alarm.

'It was Mrs Desmond's brother. He—he came to settle up. And should you answer the door to him again tell him he's unwelcome here. Don't ever let him in this house again.'

Alicia listened aghast to her daughter's bitter, unsteady voice, unrecognisable as that of her carefree, equable child.

'Did you meet him at the party?' she asked gently.

Hester laughed shortly. 'Yes. I suppose you could say that.'

'And he obviously offended you in some way.'

'Now that you can say, Mother—except that it's the understatement of the year!'

CHAPTER THREE

HESTER paused in her pacing to look at the clock. Three in the morning. Life at its lowest ebb. She thought about more coffee, then decided against it. She was already shaky and restless from the volume consumed so far, coupled with the painful reminiscences that had brought her to her feet restlessly. She made herself sit down again in a corner of the sofa, her head resting on her arm as she gazed unseeingly into the artificial flames of the gas fire. What a time she'd given her mother these past few years. Alicia was a gentle, effacing type of personality in one way, but in another indomitable, a quiet tower of strength in any crisis until today. Jo's disappearance, however, was something else. Gossip, worry, anxiety, none of these had made any difference to Alicia over the past six years until the agony of realising Jo, her darling grandchild, was—was what, thought Hester. Lost? Stolen? In the hundredth prayer uttered during the night she implored God to watch over her child, assuring Him childishly that she appreciated how busy He was, and how many people needed His attention, but could He please look out for one Josephine Alicia Ransome, who was only five years old.

Hester clamped down on a tendency to go to pieces, and deliberately turned her thoughts back to the reasons for Jo's appearance in the world. John Ransome had proved to be the type of man not easily discouraged by one dimissal from the house. The following morning a great bouquet of yellow chrysanthemums had arrived for Hester, with a card that said 'Abjectly, J.L.R.'. Abjectly! The nerve of the man, thought Hester, and dumped the flowers angrily in the

38

kitchen sink. It was left to Alicia to arrange them in a pewter jar on the hall table.

'Your mother said this Ransome man offended you pretty thoroughly at the Desmond party,' observed Lucy, reading the card with unashamed interest. 'What did he do, for heaven's sake?'

Hester refused to be drawn, and went on with the tricky job of making a pineapple Pavlova. With raised eyebrows at Mrs Price, Lucy tactfully changed the subject. Next day, however, Camilla Desmond came to see Hester to pay her bill, and shower her with her own personal apologies.

'I can't tell you how frightfully sorry I am,' she said, scarlet with embarrassment. 'I mean, really, how could John have been such a crass idiot? I feel utterly dreadful about the whole thing. It's so awful for you—I mean, if I hadn't insisted on your staying the night——'

Hester interrupted the flow hastily, assuring Camilla that she bore her no ill-will, and Camilla responded with fervent gratitude and two very welcome orders for buffet suppers from friends impressed by the meal at her party. As far as Hester was concerned that was the end of the affair. She heard no more from John Ransome, and relaxed for the rest of the week, only to find him on her doorstep one evening. She promptly tried to shut the door in his face, but a foot in an expensive shoe defeated her object, and before she could prevent it he was inside the house, tall and determined, blocking her escape in the narrow hall.

'Can't you leave me alone?' she demanded, breathing hard. 'I thought you'd done the decent thing and made a graceful exit.'

'I did, but only as far as Paris on business.' His bright, searching eyes scanned her face with unnerving intensity. 'How are you?'

'Just fine! Or at least I would be if left in peace.'

There was an unfriendly silence, while they eyed each other warily.

'My sister refuses to speak to me,' he said finally.

'Really.' Hester looked away, tapping her foot impatiently.

'I came to ask you out to dinner,' he said without preamble. Hester stared at him in amazement. 'I hoped you'd be free as it's Sunday,' he went on.

'Me?' she said scornfully. 'Break bread with you? Never in a *month* of Sundays. Goodbye, Mr Ransome.' She tried to brush past him to open the door, but he barred her way. 'This is an impossible situation to be in, Miss Price. If we'd met in the usual way——'

Hester let out an unwilling little laugh. Their formality seemed so absurd.

'You find me amusing?' he asked.

'Not you. Us. So stupidly polite with our "Miss" and "Mr": Ludicrous.'

'Then please call me John,' he said at once.

Hester's spark of humour died a sudden death.

'Oh no, Mr Ransome,' she said deliberately. 'I was speaking theoretically. Nothing's changed. My feelings towards you remain the same. I'm just calmer about the whole thing, that's all. And now goodbye.'

He gave her a look like the burn of an icecube stuck to the skin, and went. Good, thought Hester with satisfaction. That's the end of that. Again she was mistaken. After a while there was no point in deluding herself. The story was to have a sequel. When the hideous fears became certainty she was appalled, and ultimately unable to hide her dilemma from Alicia and Lucy. Cordon bleu cooking proved to be the worst of occupations for someone suffering not only from morning sickness, but a nausea that persisted every minute of the day. Lucy was blunt.

'You don't play around, so you must know who's responsible.'

'Yes,' said Alicia urgently. 'How did it happen?'

'In the usual way,' answered Hester wearily, and gave them some of the details.

'Wow! No wonder you were offended,' whistled Lucy. 'What now?'

'Not much option. I'd better get myself to the doctor and sign on for the maternity ward, I suppose.' Hester's attempt at insouciance was a miserable failure, and she sprinted to the bathroom to part with her lunch. When she returned to the kitchen Lucy coughed awkwardly.

'Have you thought of—well, you know——' she cast an uneasy glance at Alicia.

Hester nodded, her mouth wry.

'I've thought of it all right. *Ad nauseam*, if you'll pardon the pun. But I couldn't possibly, so that's it. There's not much alternative.'

Alicia's taut features relaxed, and she hugged her daughter to her, as if in protection from all comers.

'Aren't you shattered by the prospect of an illegitimate grandchild?' asked Hester shakily, returning the hug.

'It's not what I'd have chosen for you,' answered Alicia honestly, 'but it's our business entirely; nothing to do with anyone else. Present company excepted, Lucy dear,' she added, and went away to put the kettle on, as she usually did at times of crisis.

Glad that her secret was shared, Hester felt marginally happier in mind at least, though physically worse with each passing day. The doctor gave her iron tablets, advised plenty of rest and told her to drink soda water for the nausea, none of which did much good, particularly when a day or so later John Ransome arrived with his sister Camilla as insurance against non-admittance to the Price household. Lucy had apparently felt it her duty to inform Camilla of Hester's predicament. This, in turn, had prompted Camilla to speak to her brother for the first time since her party, and reluctantly agree to accompany him to see Hester.

The occasion, a very unhappy one, proved to be only a preliminary skirmish in a series of long, exhausting battles between Hester and John, which eventually

developed into a war of attrition where no one was
the victor. There would be the wedding John insisted
on as the only means of reparation he could make,
but as far as Hester was concerned that was all.
There was to be no marriage. By the time this
conclusion was reached Hester was very unwell
indeed, and she was married and hospitalised almost
in the same breath, suffering from a toxic condition
which was likely to keep her in hospital for the
duration of her pregnancy. In one way this tempered
the irregularity of their situation for both John and
Hester. Alicia, Camilla and Lucy, together with one
or two of Hester's other friends, all visited the private
room where she languished, waiting for the interminable time to pass. After a while she was
considerably improved, but not enough to be allowed
home. John came to see her each weekend for an
hour on Saturday evenings, and slightly longer on
Sundays, and at first these sessions were difficult,
trying for both of them. He brought her exquisite
flowers, hothouse fruit and the latest best-selling
novels, and made an effort at normal conversation
which sometimes proved too much for Hester. The
blue shadows beneath her eyes intensified as she tried
to control the animosity she still felt every time she
laid eyes on this attractive, charming man who, in
one negligent moment, had turned her life topsy-turvy.
John Ransome knew very well how his hostile bride
was feeling, but never once allowed her to suggest he
stopped coming. He talked determinedly on a variety
of impersonal topics, keeping her abreast of current
affairs, and to alleviate her boredom installed a video
recorder in the private room he was paying for. He
brought her videos of the latest films, including two
operas, to her delight, and never once overstepped the
line Hester had drawn between them with such
emphasis.

Surprised and anxious about John's visits in the

beginning, Alicia relaxed somewhat as time passed, particularly as Hester's health gradually improved. Then one weekend John was unable to visit, due to a business trip to the continent. The others made up the deficiency, but Hester found to her surprise that she missed not only the stimulation of male conversation, but John's physical presence itself, the actual sight of him leaning back in the chair drawn up to her bedside.

The business trip took longer than anticipated. It was three weeks before John's tall figure finally appeared in the doorway of Hester's room, and she smiled at him in spontaneous welcome, openly pleased to see him. The privacy of her room had ruled out the need for face-saving demonstrations of affection between them, but this time when John sat down by the bed he took her thin white hand in his and squeezed it gently, then gave her a small pile of parcels to unpack, to make up for his prolonged absence.

Hester exclaimed with delight as she unwrapped an exquisite silk nightgown with a matching peignoir, a box of handmade chocolates, and then another box, leather this time, which opened to reveal a travelling chess set. Hester thanked John, sincerely pleased with the gifts, though rather nonplussed at the chess set.

'I don't play,' she said apologetically.

'I know. Your mother told me.' John drew up his chair briskly. 'I'll teach you.' His even white teeth showed in a rather smug smile of satisfaction, and Hester smiled back, amused.

'I'm not very strong on patience,' she warned him.

'Then cultivating a little will be very beneficial for you. I'm an expert on the subject.' John's eyes were quizzical, and not sure which subject he meant, Hester settled down to learn the moves with as much concentration as she could muster. To her surprise she found the game fascinating, and felt keen disappointment when it was time for John to leave. She looked up at him in appeal as he stood up promptly at the usual time.

'Couldn't you stay a little longer? I'm only just getting the hang of it a little.'

John stood arrested, his face carefully blank, then he shook his head in regret. 'You look very tired, Hester. Long enough for the first lesson, I think.' He took her hand gently, as if he expected it to disintegrate at his touch.

'But you won't be here now for a week!' Hester's voice was perilously near tears, and annoyed with herself for being childish in her disappointment. 'Sorry,' she added gruffly, and tapped the slight bulge of her stomach beneath the covers. 'It's his fault I behave like a spoilt child sometimes. I'll have words with him about it when he arrives.'

John put out his hand and touched her hair, which had grown longer during her stay in hospital.

'I'll visit as often as you like, when I'm here in the U.K.,' he said, and cleared his throat. 'I kept to twice a week because I thought—no, I damn well knew I wasn't exactly welcome.'

'You weren't,' said Hester bluntly. 'But I've grown out of that. Please come whenever you can, I don't think there's any limit up in this wing.' A sudden colour rose in her pale cheeks, and her eyes dropped. 'I've never thanked you properly for arranging all this luxury for me.'

'It seemed the very least I could do.'

'No it wasn't. It's costing you a great deal of money—and I'm grateful,' she said with difficulty, her fingers pleating and unpleating the sheet.

'Hester——' John stopped as one of the nurses popped her head round the door, and whatever he had been about to say was converted into a conventional leave-taking.

John duly arranged his hours to suit Alicia, and came every evening to carry on the chess lessons. Hester looked forward to them eagerly, enjoying the battle of wits with him once she had enough grasp of the game to provide him with a measure of opposition, and the ward sister made no objection as long as her patient was settled down for the night at a reasonable hour. Then came an evening when Hester was tired, unable to play. The baby was due in a few weeks and she had some days when she felt very much worse than others. He drew his chair close to the bed and took her hand in his.

'What is it, Hester? What does the doctor say?'

She smiled, her green eyes unnaturally bright in the pallor of her fine-boned face. 'He doesn't say very much to me at all, just told me to take it easy today. Which is a pity—I was supposed to be in the ward judo finals tonight.'

John grinned, a look of tenderness on his face that for the first time struck some answering chord in Hester.

'They'll have to do without you this time, Mrs Ransome.'

Her eyes flickered.

'Sounds strange to me even now. When I first came in here I forgot to answer to it the first week or so.'

'Are you used to it now?'

'For an expectant mother it has more of a ring to it than Miss Price, I suppose.'

The fleeting moment of rapport vanished, and John drew away, leaning back in his chair while he told her about his next trip abroad the following week. Hester listened absently, her eyes on his face as he talked, struck as always by the oddity of their situation.

'Will you miss me?' he asked lightly, his grey eyes mocking.

'Yes, of course. I'll miss my chess lessons.' She widened her own eyes at him in exaggerated admiration. 'You're clever at rather a lot of things, aren't you?'

'Oh very. Jack-of-all-trades, that's me.'

'Not applicable. That means master of none—and

that most certainly isn't true in your case.' She put her head on one side. 'I like the Jack bit, though. Does anyone ever call you Jack?'

'No. Why?'

'I think I shall call you Jack. Shall you mind?' She stretched a little then caught her breath.

'What is it?' He jumped up in alarm. 'Are you in pain? Shall I call someone?'

Hester shook her head, her eyes dancing.

'Just the little newcomer doing a spot of rock and roll—perfectly routine. Does it all the time. Gets a bit more energetic some times than others, that's all.'

John stayed later than usual, uneasy about Hester's rather fey mood, and left only when discreetly requested by the night nurse, who remained in the room as he made his farewells. Aware of her interest John stooped and kissed Hester's cheek with what she took to be admirably simulated tenderness.

'Goodnight, darling, I'll be back in five days' time. Be good.'

'Chance would be a fine thing! Have fun in Italy. Goodnight—Jack.'

He grinned down into her eyes, then straightened and went from the room with a wave of his hand, and a pleasant nod to the appreciative nurse. Hester submitted to her nightly settling down routine absently, thinking how surprised the nurse would be if she knew that the chaste kiss on the cheek was the first real caress exchanged between Mr and Mrs Ransome. One could hardly count the torrid anonymous onslaught in the dark of Camilla Desmond's guest-room. Hester's face grew so hot at the thought Nurse Morris grew concerned and took her temperature again to make sure all was well.

Contrary to his promise John failed to return in five days. The evening he was due to visit Camilla appeared again instead, looking wan and unhappy, and with Alicia in tow. Hester smiled rather blankly.

'Hello, Camilla—I wasn't expecting you today. And why are you back again Mother? Jack's coming tonight.'

'Actually, no,' said Camilla miserably. 'He isn't—I mean, he can't, darling. He was on a car journey from Rome to Milan and there was a pile-up on the autostrada—Hester!' In consternation she rushed with Alicia to support Hester, who went white as the sheet and began to breathe heavily. Camilla stood back, wringing her hands while Hester panted for a moment, then lay back against her mother's shoulder, her eyes fixed on her sister-in-law's face.

'Is he——'

'He's only knocked about a bit,' Camilla assured her hurriedly. 'Honestly, darling, just bruises, broken arm and a bit shaken up. He was relatively lucky, really, Laura came off much worse; concussion, broken leg . . .' she trailed off, stricken, a hand to her mouth.

'And just who is Laura?' asked Hester coolly.

'Hasn't John——?' Camilla threw a hunted glance at Alicia, then stumbled on. 'She's his fiancée actually, no, I mean she used to be, she's his assistant now. She was before, of course, only now he's married, I mean, she isn't—his fiancée, that is. Oh gosh—Hester!'

Camilla pressed the bell frantically at Alicia's signal, as once more Hester was gripped by pain, and the ward sister came at once and took command, banishing the visitors from the room.

'A bit early yet, isn't it, Sister?' gasped Hester, dismayed. 'Must be a false alarm, surely!'

'I don't think so,' said Sister calmly, and stood taking Hester's pulse. She smiled drily. 'Babies make a habit of arriving at their own convenience, I'm afraid. Besides, you can't be sure to the day, now can you?'

'I can,' Hester assured her. 'Almost to the exact minute in fact, to be indelicate.'

And then she was completely overtaken by events. She forgot everything, her searing stab of jealousy about the unknown Laura included, as the other more overwhelming, unrelenting process took over, rendering her oblivious of anything but the agonising effort needed to bring her baby into the world.

It was over a week before John Lauder Ransome was able to visit his wife and new daughter. His arm in a sling, a black eye giving him an oddly raffish look, he hung over the cot, gazing in wonder at the little scrap of humanity his own moment of blind instinct had brought into the world. Hester sat on a chair by the window watching him, her face drawn and colourless above a long wool dressing gown which had an air of the cloister in its dark blue severity.

'She's beautiful,' said John simply, and looked up, smiling. 'And you, Hester? Are you fully recovered? I humbly apologise for not being on hand when I was needed.'

'Hardly your fault,' she murmured politely. 'And you weren't needed.'

John frowned as he recognised a return to hostilities.

'So we're back to square one again.'

Hester regarded him with wide, blank eyes.

'Had you hoped for progression, then?' she asked without interest, then shrank back in her chair as John crossed the room to stand over her, an intensity in his grey eyes that made her wary.

'I have a house not far from Burford,' he said evenly, 'fairly near Camilla's place in fact. It will have a fantastic garden when it's completed, ideal for a child. The house isn't even decorated yet, you can choose what you like in the way of furniture, colour schemes— do your own thing entirely. No, please,' as Hester was about to answer. 'Don't reject the idea out of hand. At least give it the benefit of a few minutes thought.'

Hester looked at him consideringly. He was very pale and the black eye, instead of being comic, seemed to add a note of urgency to the appeal he was making. She turned away, wondering wryly what it would be like if they ever spent time together when both of them were in the best of health. Aware that John had returned to hang in wonder over the baby's cot, Hester stared in silence at the by-pass far below, shielded from the noise of its traffic by the double glazed window of her private room. Presumably that was how life would be with John, protected from life's worries by the cushion of his wealth. She was tempted, so very tempted. Just to imagine having a free hand to decorate a house any way one wanted—who could fail to be tempted! She had a sudden absurd vision of herself in wide-brimmed hat and floating dress delicately gathering flowers in some manicured garden, the baby gurgling in a lace-trimmed bassinet nearby. The allure of the prospect was powerful. Shamefully so. Not just of pottering in John's garden and concocting elegant meals in his kitchen, but even, God help her, of sleeping in his bed. The hitherto unsuspected sybarite in Hester frankly fancied the whole idea, but only if John were motivated by love rather than duty. However, being a man of principle, she was quite certain he was acting purely from a sense of duty. And duty would be a trying house-guest for life, however luxurious the home. It was best to face the cold truth here and now. John quite plainly had a yearning for fatherhood, and the only way he could fulfil it was to include the baby's mother in the deal. Hester's face set with iron resolve as she added the final objection to her mental list.

'Well? Have you made your mind up?' John's voice broke in on her musings. He had left the baby to stand close to Hester near the window. 'You don't have to make a decision right now,' he went on. 'Sleep on it if you like.'

Hester kept her back turned, and said nothing.

'For God's sake say something, Hester!'

At the harsh urgency in his voice she turned to face him, her eyes cool and unemotional.

'Very well, I will. Where exactly does Laura figure in your plans for the future?'

John sighed impatiently, a tiny pulse beating at the corner of his mouth. 'I admit I should have told you about her sooner. Cam is practically beside herself with misery for blurting out about Laura to you. She's convinced she shocked you into premature labour.'

'Oh she mustn't be sorry. I'm grateful, truly. In fact my daughter's early arrival makes the whole thing so much easier for me when I go home. My respectability totally upheld.' Hester smiled at him with delicate malice. 'People in Orchard Crescent tend to be very un-liberated about that sort of thing.'

'Are you telling me you intend to pick up my daughter and disappear with her from my life?' John said through stiff lips. He winced as he moved his arm restively in the sling.

'Does it hurt? Was it badly broken?' asked Hester politely.

'The joint had to be pinned, that's why I was held up—what the hell does it matter!' John gripped her wrist with his good hand and drew her to her feet, close against him, his face bent to hers. 'I'm proposing, for want of a better word, Hester. I know it's a bit late in the day for that, now we're married, but I want the little one—and you, of course—to come and live with me. I'm in a position to take good care of you both. My company is successful, I'm relatively well off; you'll want for nothing, either of you.' His eyes went to the sleeping infant. 'I had no idea how much being a father would affect me—and I want her, Hester.'

'She is merely the result of an accident, John Ransome,' said Hester, the words clipped and hard, like pebbles tossed in a tin. 'A few fleeting moments you were barely conscious were happening do not qualify you to be a father. Not in the way I'm her mother. All the months of sickness and lying around in here were mine—and worth every second now she's here, but I really don't see why I have to share her with you! Unless, of course, you feel I owe you for my hospital fees and the marriage licence, in which case I can soon pay you back once I start working again.'

'God in heaven!' John scowled down at her in outraged disbelief, his fingers bruising her wrist. 'Have I been deluding myself?' he demanded. 'I thought we'd grown closer together, Hester, over the past month or two. It was *your* idea I visited you more often!'

'Not one of my better ones.' Hester winced and tried to pull her arm free. John loosened his fingers a little but still kept hold of her hand. 'I was bored,' she added cruelly, 'and I enjoyed pitting my wits against you at chess, but I don't look on you as a husband, and I didn't know anything about Laura. Which you must admit is rather odd, since I gather you were actually *living* together at the time.'

He dropped her hand as if it stung him, and turned on his heel to stare blindly through the window. There was a nerve-fraying silence.

'I don't know why I bother,' he said at last, his voice so bitter it was barely recognisable. 'It's patently obvious that whatever I do to make amends, as far as you're concerned I'm no better than a common rapist.' He took in a deep breath. 'Not, I'm sure, that it will be of any interest to you, but just for the records Laura and I have never lived together.'

'I'm really not very concerned——'

'You should be. You brought it up!'

'Very well then,' said Hester coldly. 'I must admit to some curiosity about the lady. She must surely have suffered something of a shock to find out you were visiting an expectant mother in hospital at the same time you were conducting a romance with her.'

John had himself well in hand again, and turned narrowed, satiric eyes on her disdainful face.

'She took it in her stride. Which is hardly surprising, when the social side of my relationship with her ended from the time I met you. Before I even knew you were pregnant.'

Hester raised a sceptical eyebrow.

'I find that very hard to believe.'

He shrugged, his face impassive.

'The truth often is. And we did not exactly live together, as I said. We shared a bed occasionally, yes, but otherwise we kept to our separate establishments, and we have certainly never been engaged. That's just Camilla's euphemism for the type of relationship Laura and I enjoyed.'

'But she still works for you.'

'Yes, of course. She's damned good at her job, and we remain good friends.'

'An idyllic arrangement,' observed Hester acidly. 'And how is she now? I gather she came off worse in the accident?'

'Yes. She was in front with the driver. Luckily her injuries were all minor, and she hopes to get back to work in a month's time. I'll be glad to have her back.' John eyed her coolly. 'It might interest you to know that since I met you I have neither taken a woman out socially nor slept with one.'

Hester recoiled.

'What possible interest can that be to me!'

'God knows,' he said wearily, passing a hand over his eyes. 'You were interested enough in Laura. I thought you might like the entire record straight. You are rather a difficult person to please, Hester.'

Suddenly an indignant wail sounded behind them, and John sprang over to the cot, his face anxious as he looked at the furious red face of his daughter.

'What's the matter with her?' he asked. 'Is she ill?'

Hester smiled faintly.

'No. It's suppertime that's all, and she demands punctuality.'

'May I watch while she has her bottle?'

Hester's eyes dropped, colour rising in her cheeks.

'I was rotten at being pregnant, but I'm a whiz at feeding my daughter in the old-fashioned way, to my surprise, so if you don't mind I need a little privacy.'

'Yes, of course.' John's colour matched hers as he made hurriedly for the door. He turned to watch Hester lift the baby from the cot, the noise abating at once. 'Will you think about my suggestion, Hester?'

She held the baby's head close against her shoulder, rocking her gently as she returned his look very directly.

'No Jack. We're just strangers, really, linked solely by the accident of Jo's birth. It wouldn't work.'

'Is that what you call her? Jo?' he asked quietly.

For a moment Hester's resolution almost wavered, then it hardened again.

'Yes. Jo.' As if the sound of her name were a signal, the hungry baby set up her clamour again, and Hester had to raise her voice to make herself heard. 'It's checkmate, Jack. My mind is made up.'

CHAPTER FOUR

THE Hester of five years later wished drearily she had the same diamond-bright conviction. Seeing John Ransome again tonight had been disturbing, raking up old ashes long considered dead. He was different, changed—colder and more introverted than the man who had married her. His company had gone on from strength to strength in the age of the computer, and now he was very much a man to be reckoned with, both professionally and personally, totally in command, except in one area. His daughter obviously meant a great deal more to him than Hester had ever allowed herself to believe.

As the hours dragged by she thought wistfully it would have been comforting to ask John to stay to share her vigil, but he had become distant and unapproachable during the intervening years. When she had insisted on a divorce as soon as legally possible after Jo's birth he had tried to change her mind. Obstinate little fool, reflected Hester. Her whole persona must have been knocked out of true by the trauma of Jo's birth to make her take off like a rocket when she found out about Laura. Such a violent reaction must have been the result of post-natal blues. Not only had she suffered such an astonishing attack of jealousy, but the hurt had gone deep to find out that John had entirely omitted any mention of Laura's mere existence, let alone his relationship with her. Camilla's ill-timed disclosure had been all the more startling since it came at the very stage where Hester's feelings for John had been undergoing a gradual change from hostility to warmth, and a certain dangerous dependence. Eventually John Ransome's pride had baulked at any further persuasion, and Hester had been granted her wish to be free of him. Latterly she had even been moved to enough generosity to allow him to see his daughter for one whole day every fortnight. And in return John paid Hester a generous allowance she never touched, plus the fees and expenses for the very upmarket school he had insisted on for Jo.

During the dragging night hours Hester looked the truth in the face for the first time, and cared very little for what she saw. The hardest fact to accept was that her chosen way of life wasn't up to much, even though she had been so immovably insistent on it. In her innermost heart she knew very well that all those months in hospital had wrought a gradual softening in her feelings towards John, even though she was convinced he had married her solely from a feeling of guilt. Without even realising it she had grown to care for John Ransome, able to see him not as an unthinking brute who had wrecked her life, but as a considerate, attentive man with a fine intellect and more than his fair share of physical attributes. If he had asked her to make their marriage a real one only one day earlier both their lives might have been different. But before John could get back from Italy fate had intervened in the shape of the Sunday newspapers. Propped up against pillows in her expensive private room, her daughter snuffling and grunting contentedly in the cot at the foot of the bed, Hester had stared, dismayed, at an article in one of the colour supplements. It was one of a series on up and coming personalities in the business world. This one was a profile on John Lauder Ransome himself, plus the woman in his life, his assistant, Miss Laura Verney, a groomed and gleaming brunette, as the photograph showed, with a string of high-powered qualifications to back up her looks—not so much a girl Friday as a woman for all seasons. John's face had looked back at her from the page, level-eyed and remote and suddenly beyond reach. Hester had looked long at first one face then the other before reaching for a mirror to study her own.

The face she saw was pale, the skin and hair lifeless, her eyes inanimate and dull. With a grimace she put away the mirror, and with it all the half-formed, unacknowledged stirrings of her heart. Merely to hear about Laura had been bad enough, but to see her in glorious technicolour, actually hinted at as the power behind John's throne, was too much. Hester recognised defeat when she saw it. By the time John had arrived with his proposal she was armoured against him, utterly convinced that a strong sense of duty was his only possible motivation, and she had sent him away and shut him out of her life.

This same life needed rather a lot of re-organisation. Lucy, unable to continue with their catering service in Hester's prolonged absence, had gone off to London to teach others to cook instead of doing it herself, so as soon as Jo was weaned Hester searched for work she could do alone, and at home. By a stroke of great good fortune she landed the order for supplying desserts to a local hotel, and soon her life became a routine which revolved around kitchen, nursery, food wholesalers, and quiet evenings with Alicia in front of the television.

The sudden shrill of the telephone shocked Hester out of her abstraction, sending her flying to the study, the receiver shaking in her unsteady hand as she picked it up.

'Hello,' she said hoarsely.

There was silence at the other end of the line for a moment, then a whisper sounded in her straining ear, almost inaudible.

'What did you say?' cried Hester wildly. 'Who is this? Is anyone there?'

'Jo . . . back garden . . .' came the stifled whisper in response, and the line went dead.

'Hester—who was it?' Alicia ran in, tying her dressing gown round her with trembling fingers, and colliding with her daughter in the doorway. Hester put her aside without ceremony.

'I don't know, but I think they said Jo's in the back garden.' She ran through the hall to the kitchen, pausing only long enough to collect a torch before wrenching open the back door into the long, narrow garden at the back of the house, Alicia hard on her heels. Hester flew down the path, flashing the beam of light in all directions, but there was no sign of Jo. Almost sobbing in her anxiety she unlocked the gate in the garden wall and nearly fell over the bundle lying directly outside. Her heart flopped over in her breast as she shone the torch on the inert little figure in unfamiliar anorak and jeans, a knitted cap pulled down over the forehead. Alicia gave a stifled little cry and caught the torch Hester tossed to her, watching as Hester swept the still little form up into her arms, then following as she ran back into the house. Hester hugged the small limp body close, a terrible fear tightening her chest. In silence Alicia watched, white to the lips, as in the warmth of the living room Hester tenderly removed the knitted cap, giving a gasp of surprise as she saw Jo's hair, which had been cropped close to her head like a boy's above the closed eyes.

'Turn on more lights please, Mother,' she ordered, brusque in her anxiety. Alicia obeyed, and ran for a blanket, relaxing a little when she came back and tucked it round Jo.

'She's breathing quite normally, Hester,' she said reassuringly.

Hester nodded, her eyes glued to the still white face, deeply worried by the blue marks beneath the closed lids. 'She's sedated or—or drugged, I think.'

'I'll ring the doctor,' said Alicia promptly.

'Yes, please—then Jack, if you would, love, the number's by the 'phone.'

'Heavens yes, of course.'

Hester sat rocking her child against her, talking to her gently, trying to penetrate Jo's unnatural stillness.

'Come on, Baby, talk to Mother, you're home and safe now. Wake up, Jo, try for me, don't be lazy. Come on, poppet, wake up!'

For a moment Hester imagined she saw the lashes flutter, but otherwise Jo lay still and unresponsive in her arms, only a very slight warmth in the little body giving her any reassurance.

Alicia came back quickly.

'Dr Fenner's on his way, and by this time so is John.' She put out a hand to touch Hester's. 'He must have been right alongside the telephone. It barely had time to ring before he answered.'

Hester nodded wearily.

'It's been a long night. What time is it?'

'Five-ish.'

'God! I wonder how long she's been out there in the dark and the cold.'

'Who gave the message, darling?'

'They didn't identify themselves. I couldn't even tell if the voice was male or female—it was just a hoarse whisper saying where Jo was, then the line went dead.'

When the doctor arrived he heard the story of Jo's disappearance with concern. He examined the little body thoroughly after Hester stripped it of its alien clothes, lifting up the flaccid eyelids and taking her pulse.

'Some form of sedation has been administered orally,' he said. 'No sign of a hypodermic needle puncture anywhere. Don't worry. Pulse strong, colour not too bad, she couldn't have been left in the cold very long. She'll do very well now, but give me a ring if you need me. I'll call back tomorrow.' He got up and snapped his bag shut, yawning a little. 'Just keep her warm and she'll come out of it naturally in her own good time. And try to relax, ladies—Jo looks better than either of you.'

Hester smiled her grateful thanks and turned back to Jo, dressing her in warm pyjamas and wool dressing gown, tugging thick socks on the limp feet before wrapping the little body in the blanket and cuddling it close. Suddenly she felt gloriously happy, the relief bubbling inside her like champagne as her mother came back from seeing off the doctor.

'O.K. then, Mrs Price. Do your stuff with the kettle. Let's have some coffee and perhaps some toast. Suddenly I feel hungry.'

Alicia's face lit up and she darted off to obey. Only minutes later the doorbell rang and Hester looked at her watch in astonishment. John Ransome must have broken the sound barrier to arrive so rapidly. Alicia let him in and Hester stood up with Jo in her arms as John strode into the room, his hair untidy and his eyes bloodshot. He looked unfamiliar, oddly younger despite his haggard face, dressed in a suede battle blouse and cord trousers.

'Hester, thank God,' he said huskily, and swept her into his arms, child and all, holding them both in a convulsive grip. Hester could feel the tension of his body against hers and her throat constricted in sympathy. After only a moment he drew back to hang over Jo's unconscious face, frowning and anxious.

'Where was she? Is she all right? What did the doctor say? Let me hold her, Hester.'

She could afford to be generous now she had Jo back. Hester surrendered the child into John's arms and sat down beside him on the sofa while she told him what the doctor said.

'I couldn't tell who it was on the telephone,' she went on, 'not even if the voice were male or female. It just whispered that Jo was in the back garden, then the person hung up, so I ran outside with the torch.' Her face hardened. 'She was dumped outside the garden gate in the lane running behind it, frozen stiff and unconscious like this.'

The look on John's face was ugly.

'I'll find out who did it one way or another, you can

be sure of that. I rang the police. They'll be here shortly.'

'Oh, of course. I'd forgotten. I suppose they'll need to know all the details.' Hester gave him a tired smile. 'Silly of me to bother about something trifling I know, but just look what they've done to her hair, Jack. All her curls are gone.'

'But *she's* back, Hester. The hair will grow again.' John put out a hand to grip hers, his touch consoling, as though he understood her regret over the curls, aware of the emotional imbalance she was experiencing. There was a moment of complete harmony between them while they looked steadily at each other, then John looked up quickly, his face remorseful as Alicia came into the room with a tray.

'I do apologise, Alicia. I just barged past you without so much as a by your leave, or even hello.'

'And who could blame you,' she answered cheerfully. 'Now *this* time both of you try to eat some toast and drink some coffee before there are any more interruptions.'

It should have been odd, tucking into the hot buttered toast over the sleeping form of the child, but neither Hester nor John felt any constraint as they enjoyed the impromptu breakfast with an appetite sharpened by sheer euphoria. Alicia poured out for them, quiet as usual, her happiness radiating from her as she gazed almost continually at her granddaughter's face, apparently afraid Jo would disappear if she looked away.

'Are you sure she's all right?' asked John, frowning down at the still small face. 'The doctor was quite definite in his diagnosis, I suppose?'

'Of course he was!' Hester's hackles rose for a moment, then she relaxed. He had a right to be apprehensive, after all.

'Jo's colour is much better than when Hester brought her in,' Alicia reassured him, and refilled his coffee cup. John sighed, and thrust his free hand through his hair.

'I'm sorry. It's been such an interminable wait. I wanted to ring you during the night,' he said to Hester, 'but I thought it best to leave the line free. Why, for God's sake, would they just bring her back, do you think?'

'Search me!' Hester gazed dreamily at Jo's sleeping face. 'I'm merely thankful they did.'

'But what motivation is there in taking someone's child away for a day then bringing her back with no demand for money in exchange?' John asked, baffled.

The police had no theories to offer, either. They arrived a little later and heard all the details from Hester, took away the clothes Jo had been dressed in, and that was that. Inspector Mason would return during the day to hear if Jo herself could throw any light on her abduction when she woke. After the police had gone Hester gave an almighty yawn, exhaustion swamping her now that the crisis was over.

'You look shattered,' said John. 'Why don't you get some sleep?'

'I want to stay with Jo,' she said at once.

'Why don't you *both* get some sleep?' interposed Alicia with unusual authority. 'I'll sit with Jo and the moment she wakes I'll call you both. You can rest on my bed, John—after you've both put Jo to bed.'

John's face relaxed as he turned to Hester.

'Is that acceptable to you?'

'Why yes, of course.' Hester could hardly say anything else, even though she felt uneasy at the thought of John in the room next to hers. She could see the obvious sense of her mother's suggestion, and smiled politely, with an effort. 'We'll both be better for a rest, and it's quite possible Jo will sleep for hours yet. I'll show you her room.'

John got up carefully with his burden, smiling at Alicia.

'Thank you for the use of your room, I promise to treat it gently.'

She laughed. 'Have a good rest, John. You look terrible.'

He did too, thought Hester, as she preceded him from the living room, conscious of the look she was sure he had fixed on her shoulder-blades as he followed her up the red-carpeted staircase. She wondered if he were thinking, as she was, that this was the first time he had ever been upstairs in the house, and led the way to Jo's domain, which looked out on the quiet back garden. It was a gay little room, bright with yellow paint, the walls covered with posters and the curtains printed with racing-cars.

'Cars?' John raised his eyebrows, grinning at the unexpected choice as he laid his little daughter on the turned-down bed. Hester shrugged as she tucked Jo, dressing-gown and all, under the duvet.

'You must know she's not a doll girl by the presents you buy her.'

'Shall we say I'm just beginning to. I've had less time to get to know her than you have.' John looked at her very directly, and Hester turned on her heel and went from the room, leaving him to follow her quickly to the other end of the landing, where her own bedroom adjoined Alicia's. John paused as Hester opened her door.

'I'd like to talk to you for a moment, Hester.'

She hesitated, unwilling, but after an uncertain look towards the stairs she nodded ungraciously and motioned him to follow her into her bedroom, which still contained the narrow bed of her girlhood. Otherwise the decoration and curtains were recent, with a great deal of stark white paint to match bedcover and carpet, even the curtains white except for a muted print of waterlilies and greenery. The dustjackets of the books piled on the bedside table provided the only strident note. John stood with eyebrows raised, tall and alien in the midst of such austere femininity, an intrusive male figure in his earth-coloured jacket. He stared at his surroundings with undisguised interest, shaking his head slightly.

'So this is where you sleep, Hester. Exactly as I've pictured it.'

Her chin lifted defensively.

'I'm surprised you spare any thought at all to where I sleep.'

'Yes Hester, I'm sure you are.'

John reached out a hand and closed the door quietly, then seated himself in her white-painted rocking chair, looking at length on the taut, slender figure standing so obviously ill-at-ease near the dressing table. Hester flushed as his eyes remained on her, almost in contemplation.

'You wanted to talk,' she reminded him.

He answered with the last thing she expected.

'Is that the same dressing-gown you wore in hospital when Jo was born?'

Hester stared at him blankly.

'No. It's new. I bought it to go away on the course. The other one was a bit tatty.'

John shook his head in apparent wonder as he rocked idly back and fore.

'You must have had quite a search to find one so similar.'

'If you merely wanted to talk about my dressing-gown—riveting topic though it is, of course—could we postpone it until some other time?' Hester yawned pointedly.

'If you follow your usual pattern there probably won't be another time.' He stretched out his long legs comfortably and folded his arms, a look of annoying reason on his face. 'If it weren't for Jo's disappearance I wouldn't be here now, would I? And you contacted me over that only because you cast me for villain of the piece as usual. As for the nun-like dressing-gown, I merely thought it all of a piece with this.' He waved a hand at the room. 'It's the next best thing to an anchorite's cell, for God's sake.'

Hester turned her back, her hands in her dressing-gown pockets to hide their trembling. To elude the analytical grey eyes she concentrated on the objects on the dressing table, but they only supported his argument. There was no perfume and make up, no feminine jumble; just the small white-framed photograph of Jo, a silver box containing two or three pieces of jewellery and a white ceramic bud vase, waiting for June and the first of the Iceberg roses she kept in it in season.

'What did you expect?' she asked irritably. 'Mirrors on the ceiling? I don't like clutter.'

'I can see that,' he agreed promptly. 'You like to pare things down to the bare essentials. Nothing unnecessary like a husband, even though he's the father of your child.'

'You missed your vocation, Jack. You should have taken up psychiatry.'

He ignored her sarcasm.

'It's really quite unbelievable,' he went on. 'No one would believe that this is my first admission into your bedroom, and that the only kiss I've ever given you has been a chaste salute on the cheek.'

'Ah, but that's where you're wrong,' said Hester unwisely, and swung round to glare at him. 'You may have been too drunk to remember the other kisses, but I wasn't. There was nothing remotely chaste about those.'

John rose slowly to his feet, holding her eyes with his. Silently he moved towards her, and Hester stood rooted to the spot, her back against the dressing table with no room to retreat as he reached out and took hold of her shoulders.

'I've always felt there was a certain injustice about my lack of recall regarding that fateful night,' he said softly. 'Since you've made me pay for it ever since, in ways many and various, it seems a crying shame——'

'I've made you pay for nothing,' interrupted Hester hotly.

'Oh yes you have. No financial demands, I grant you. But in other ways. Like rationing my time with Jo so stringently.' John looked thoughtfully at her pale, frightened face. 'Scared of me, Hester? I'm not going to hurt you. Just kiss you.'

She twisted her face aside, but he caught her chin in one hand and brought her face up to meet his. He put his mouth on hers with slow deliberation and Hester struggled for a moment, then stopped. All the fight had been drained out of her by the events of the night, and her mouth was flaccid and unresponsive against his. After a moment or two John raised his head and looked at her with derision. He dropped his hands and moved back, his expression sending the colour beating to her cheeks.

'Hardly worth the bother, was it? Good night, Hester, or perhaps it's good morning.' John strolled unhurriedly from the room, closing the door behind him with exaggerated care.

Hester flopped down on the dressing table stool, angry tears trickling down her cheeks. She dashed them away impatiently and stared at herself in the mirror. Her hair was hanging down, her eyes glittering like an angry cat, and her face on fire with sheer temper. She wished urgently that John would walk back through the doorway, so she could throw something at him, attack him even, then stopped short, forcing herself to calm down. She heard Alicia quietly climbing the stairs to sit with Jo, and almost went to join her, but knew that was pointless. She jumped to her feet and stripped off the offending dressing-gown, hurling it to the floor in a defiant gesture of untidiness to the suddenly offensive order of the cool room, then she climbed into bed to stew over John's unforgivable words. What had he expected? A passionate love-scene on top of such a nerve-wracking night? She gritted her teeth, trying vainly to relax. Her body yearned for sleep, but her mind was jumping about like popcorn in a pan. John's comment rang on in her ears, acting like salt on an open wound. After an interval of tossing and turning she heard the door open cautiously and footsteps approaching the bed.

'Get out!' she spat, and heaved over to turn on the light, looking up appalled into the startled face of her mother.

'I thought you might find it hard to sleep, and wondered if you wanted a drink,' said Alicia. 'But if you're in that frame of mind I'll just get back to my post.'

Hester sat up, rubbing a hand over her face.

'Sorry, Mother. I must have been dreaming.'

Alicia's eyes flickered, but she merely said 'Jo's still out for the count, darling, so do try to get some rest. You look worn to shreds, Hester.'

Hester's sorely-tried sense of humour reasserted itself as she settled herself down to sleep. Her ego was certainly taking a beating tonight, one way and another. A wry smile lingered on her face as she stretched out with a sigh, wondering why the truth always hurt so much. Both John and Alicia had been absolutely right.

She seemed to have slept for only a moment before she woke to violent shaking and an excited voice chanting in her ear.

'Wakey, wakey, wake up lazy Mummy.'

Hester sat up with a jerk, laughing with joy at the sight of the small figure in striped pyjamas bouncing on the end of the bed, the terrible haircut giving Jo the look of a wicked little boy. Jo threw herself into her mother's outstretched arms, and they hugged each other hard, the tears streaming unashamedly down Hester's face on to Jo's shorn head until the child drew away, looking accusingly at her mother's wet cheeks.

'Mummies don't cry!'

'This one does when she's happy.' Hester assured her, and gave a great sniff. 'Am I glad to see you, Jo Ransome. How do you feel?'

The dancing green eyes clouded for a moment and Jo's mouth trembled, then her whole face lit up as John appeared in the doorway, dressed only in his cord trousers, a villainous dark blond growth of beard on his chin.

'Daddy!' shrieked Jo incredulously, and hurled herself at him like a missile, burrowing her face against John's rough cheek as his arms threatened to crack the small ribs. His jaw clenched as he held his daughter close, not saying a word. Hester cleared her throat.

'I've just been informed mummies don't cry,' she warned him huskily, hugging her knees under the covers. John gave a strangled laugh as Jo released him, rubbing her face indignantly.

'You've got prickles on your face like Herbert——'

'School hedgehog,' supplied Hester with a grin.

'I need a shave. I do apologise,' said John solemnly, now in possession of himself again. He sat down on Hester's bed, holding Jo on his knee. She beamed up at him happily.

'Do you live here now, like Belinda's daddy—and why weren't you in the car yesterday? The man said my daddy was in the car, but you weren't and it was a horrid car, and they put a blanket on my head——' she stopped for breath, scarlet with indignation.

'Jo.' John turned her face up to his seriously. 'The man told lies, darling. Think hard. I never fetch you from school, do I? I send Tyler to ring Mummy's doorbell for you every other Saturday. But only on Saturdays, never schooldays.'

Jo frowned, concentrating on what he said, gazing up at him with such trust and love Hester sat in silence as she watched them, filled with an unaccustomed feeling of guilt.

'Where did they take you, Jo?' she asked.

John met her eyes over the child's head and without a word moved to sit nearer, Jo wriggling between them like a rapturous puppy.

'Don't know.' Jo scowled from one to the other in fierce resentment. 'They made me stay under the blanket. It was horrid and smelt yucky.' She screwed up her face in disgust. 'The man carried me up some stairs when the car stopped, and I kicked him hard.'

John bit his lip, avoiding Hester's eye.

'I don't suppose he liked that very much.'

Jo shook her head.

'He wanted to smack me, but the lady said no.'

'Lady?' said Hester sharply.

'The lady in the room,' said Jo impatiently.

'What was she like?'

'Quite old—like you.'

John stifled a chuckle.

'Was she pretty, like Mummy?'

Jo wrinkled her nose.

'She had funny hair, and her jeans had holes.'

'Was she nice?'

Jo bounced on the bed, thinking hard. Finally she nodded.

'She said I was clever.'

'Why?'

''Cos I knew the number.'

Hester frowned.

'What number, darling?'

'Grandma's telephone. I told them Grandma was fetching me 'cos you were away, so they whispered a lot, then the lady left me with the man, and he took my school things off and cut my hair and I screamed.'

John shifted Jo on to his lap and put his free arm around Hester, her sudden pallor disturbing him. 'Did they hurt you, Jo?' he asked tightly. The child thought for a moment again.

'No-o,' she decided, 'but I wanted you and Mummy and Grandma, and—and I wanted to come home.' She dissolved into tears and buried her face against John's chest for a moment while he held her tightly, and Hester battled against her own tears. After a moment or two Jo recovered gamely, rubbing her tears away with her knuckles while her parents leaned against each other for support, their differences disregarded for the moment. Then something occurred to Jo and she smiled triumphantly. 'I had fish'n chips out of a bag—and they're *not* nasty like you said, Mummy.'

'You don't say,' said Hester drily. 'Well, don't imagine I'll cook them for you, Jo Ransome, just the same.'

'You don't *cook* them,' explained Jo patiently. 'You buy them in a shop!'

John laughed and squeezed her. 'Was the room big, darling?'

'No. Teeny.'

'Did it have a bed?'

'Sort of. A funny, wobbly one.' Suddenly she scowled. 'They kept calling me Jo-Jo. Stupid! I *said* I was Jo—I *told* them. My friend is Jo-Jo.'

'The little American girl,' said Hester, her eyes narrowing.

'What's Jo-Jo's other name?' asked John quickly.

Jo just shrugged, and Hester and John exchanged a look over her head.

'What else happened, sweetheart?' asked John gently.

'Lots of questions,' sighed Jo wearily. 'I told them Daddy didn't live with us and my Mummy was a cook.'

Hester caught John's eye and giggled.

'That must have thrown them!'

Jo disentangled herself and settled in front of them, cross-legged, smiling expectantly. 'Grandma's making lunch. Are you having lunch with us, Daddy?'

'Am I?' asked John unfairly, looking at Hester.

'Of course,' she said evenly, 'unless you have anything more pressing.'

'Not a thing.'

'Then that's settled.'

Jo listened to this exchange with satisfaction, then she remembered something else.

'They put jeans on me, and they made me say my name a lot of times. So I showed the lady my blazer.'

'And she saw your name and address,' said Hester thoughtfully.

'And then they shouted at each other and I cried and cried, and I couldn't stop when they said.' Jo's mouth trembled. 'They made me drink nasty-tasting coke, and I didn't like it. I choked.'

John's arm tightened on Hester's shoulders convulsively.

'What happened then, darling?'

'The lady made the man go away, and she held me on her lap.' Suddenly Jo was smiling again. 'Then I woke up in my own bed. Was it magic?'

'No. The people who took you left you here when you were sleeping,' explained Hester. 'Now hop off to the bathroom—you need a bath.'

'O.K.' said Jo happily. She paused at the door, her eyes wide and questioning. 'You will be here when I get back, Daddy?'

John jumped to his feet and tossed her up in his arms.

'Better still, I'll come and scrub your back and maybe have a wash myself—if that's all right with Mummy.' He looked at Hester over Jo's head.

'Of course,' she said, and only waited for the door to close behind them before diving out of bed to dress in jeans and shirt, pulling on her boots and making a determined effort to tame her hair. Instead of its usual knot she tied it back with a blue velvet ribbon and ran down to Alicia, who was whistling like a blackbird as she prepared vegetables to accompany the roast. She looked up with a smile as Hester caught her round the waist and hugged her until she begged for mercy.

'I sent Jo in to wake you up on her own—I thought

you'd prefer it,' Alicia said breathlessly. 'I heard a bit of the story, but you can fill me in later.'

'Jack's presiding over madam's bath at the moment.' Hester hooked her thumbs in her belt and leaned against a counter, frowning. 'It was a case of mistaken identity, I think; they thought Jo was someone else. But they can't have been so very terrible to bring her back, can they, Mother?'

'No. For which I've been giving thanks ever since her reappearance.' Alicia looked up questioningly. 'Is John staying to lunch?'

Hester nodded casually. 'I could hardly send him off without eating under the circumstances.'

'Then shouldn't you do something about your face?'

Hester wrinkled her nose, laughing, and bent over the sink to wash her face under the tap. She blotted it dry with kitchen paper. 'There. That'll do.'

'No make-up?' Alicia kept her eyes on the batter she was whisking.

'Jack is merely staying to lunch, darling, so don't start any cosy little plans on our behalf,' warned Hester.

'If I were the type to do that, dearest daughter, I would have been a great deal more vocal on the same subject more than five years ago.' Alicia's tone was unusually tart as she expelled the whisks from the electric hand beater into the sink. Hester eyed her in surprise.

'Are you saying I should have stayed married to Jack, then?'

'I am trying to say I am not the type to put my parental oar in very much at all. It's your life, Hester. You must arrange it as you think best for yourself. And for Jo.' Alicia began scraping carrots with energy, and Hester took a knife from the drawer and joined in, looking thoughtful. She cast a look at Alicia's pretty, fair-skinned face and youthful figure.

'Have you never wanted to remarry, Mother?'

'No. But I had been very happily married once

already—to someone I loved very much. I'd hate to think you were never to experience the same sort of relationship. Now; shall we have cabbage or cauliflower with the roast beef?'

'Both—as we appear to be eating Sunday lunch on Saturday!'

Alicia reached up and patted her daughter's cheek.

'I felt we needed something substantial after the horrors of last night. And as, unlike you, I am just a good plain cook, meat and veg are what you're getting.'

The meal had to be kept hanging about for a while, as Inspector Mason arrived to learn what details could be gleaned from Jo's patchy account. She was far less forthcoming with the stranger, and became distressed at more questions, and eventually John gave her into Alicia's keeping and gave a summary of Jo's description of events. After John finished the inspector gave them an interesting piece of information. Apparently one of his colleagues had been called in that morning by a colonel from the U.S. airbase. A note had been delivered to the colonel's house, instructing him to order all nuclear missiles removed from the base in return for his little daughter, who was in the sender's custody. The colonel and his wife had been out the previous evening, and the note went unnoticed until breakfast time with the rest of the mail, when the small daughter in question was sitting at the table eating her cereal.

John and Hester exchanged glances.

'What is the colonel's name, Inspector?' asked John quickly.

'Rantzen, sir, and the child's name is Josephine, though I am informed she answers to the name of Jo-Jo.'

'That's what the kidnappers kept calling *our* daughter,' exclaimed Hester.

Inspector Mason nodded. 'It would seem to be a case

of mistaken identity, Madam. The man who collected the child asked for Josephine Rantzen and the supply teacher, a very flustered lady indeed when I questioned her, handed over your little girl by mistake. She is a little hard of hearing and the names sounded the same to her, also the little American girl was not at school yesterday; a bad cold, I understand.'

'Who were the kidnappers, then?' asked John, his eyes intent.

'They called themselves "Saviours of the Earth", Mr Ransome. No commercial gain intended, I believe, merely an effort to further their cause by the strongest pressure they could devise.' The inspector shrugged, a twinkle in his eyes. 'It's to be hoped the fate of the earth lies in less inept hands! I suppose one can't condemn them entirely; they returned your little girl when they discovered their mistake. I hope she suffered no harm?'

'No,' said Hester. 'Not physically, anyway. Their worst crime was to drug Jo's drink and leave her in the cold outside at night, unless you count an atrocious haircut and an introduction to the delights of takeaway fish and chips.'

When the Inspector had left John came back from seeing him off and looked at Hester, frowning. She lay back in her chair, eyes closed, her long, slender legs stretched out in front of her in an attitude of utter weariness.

'Reaction?' he asked, standing over her.

She nodded, without opening her eyes.

'I want to apologise, Hester,' he said. Her eyes flew open, bright green with surprise.

'For kissing me, Jack?'

His eyes held an odd expression as they met hers without evasion.

'Not for kissing you. For my comment afterwards.'

'It made me mad as hell,' she said without emotion, and yawned. 'Kept me awake for quite a time. Lord,

I'm jiggered. Good thing I don't start working again until Monday.'

John's frown deepened as he looked coldly at her pale, exhausted face.

'Why must you drive yourself like this, Hester? Is the money I give you tainted in some way, that you can't bring yourself to touch it? Or does it detract from the precious independence you seem to value above everything else?'

Hester looked back at him quietly, without the instant animosity he quite obviously expected, but with an apathy in her eyes that dulled their normal clarity. 'I haven't any answers for anything at the moment, Jack,' she said flatly. 'The shock of yesterday seems to have pushed me off-centre, or something. I feel—silly of me, I suppose—but I feel more apprehensive today than I did last night.'

'Why?'

'I—I feel superstitious.' She shrugged apologetically. 'I really don't care for the way things happen to me by accident. I thought once was enough when I—when you—when I got pregnant by sheer mistake. But now Jo was actually kidnapped by the mere coincidence of her name being similar to that of another child. I loathe feeling like an ant ready to be trodden on by an elephantine stroke of fate any minute, Jack. I want to be in charge of my own destiny, not helpless in the grip of circumstances.'

John bent and pulled her to her feet.

'Come on. At the moment you're in the grip of aftermath, Hester. All your self-confidence will be back in full force by tomorrow, you can be sure. At present you're still in shock.'

'Mummy! Daddy!' Jo came hurtling into the room, a streak of flour down her sweater. 'We've been to the shop and I've helped Grandma make gravy, and she says lunch is ready, 'n I'm hungry. Please come.'

John scooped her up into his arms, his eyes laughing

as he rubbed noses with her. 'Right this minute, ma'am. Lead on Mummy, and I'll give Jo a piggy-back.'

It was warm and sunny in the big kitchen, the air heavy and tantalising with the scent of roast beef. As John carved the meat and Alicia handed vegetables and Yorkshire puddings Hester's feeling of insecurity gradually subsided, helped along by the good food, and the red wine Alicia produced as a surprise.

'Where did that come from, Mother?' asked Hester, amused. Wine was by no means one of their usual indulgences.

'I took Jo for a little walk to the off-licence while you were talking to the inspector,' said Alicia.

'I had sweets,' said Jo with satisfaction, tucking into her meal with gusto.

'And how many did you eat?' enquired her mother.

'Only one teeny-weeny one.'

Alicia smiled at her indulgently. 'I felt we had something to celebrate.'

'Amen to that.' John raised his glass.

They all drank a heartfelt toast, Jo mimicking the adults with her own glass of lemonade-diluted wine. After the meal John looked at the time and glanced at Hester, an eyebrow raised.

'Today's my usual day with Jo, Hester. Had you forgotten?'

She had. She stared at him blankly. It had gone out of her head completely. Today was the day for the fortnightly ritual John enjoyed with his daughter. She frowned and bit her lip, looking over at Jo. The child's eyes were very heavy as she languidly pushed chocolate mousse round her dish. Hester was afraid it would be open to misinterpretation if she refused to let Jo go out with her father, yet the child looked in sore need of a rest. John was very much aware of her dilemma.

'Don't worry, Hester. I think Jo needs a nap, myself, not an outing.'

'Aren't we going out then, Daddy?' Jo's eyes filled

with tears, her face crumpling beneath her raggedly cropped hair.

'You really are tired, darling,' said Alicia gently. 'Perhaps Daddy is free to take you out tomorrow instead.' She gave Hester a straight look as she stood up to clear away.

'Fine by me.' Hester was secretly relieved to have the suggestion made for her, especially when Jo's tears dried like magic as she turned hopefully to her father.

'Of course I'm free,' said John promptly, and beckoned Jo over to him, lifting her on his lap and holding her close. She leaned against him contentedly, her cheek cuddled against the smooth cashmere of his sweater. 'Perhaps we could do something different for a change,' he added.

Hester banished the little stab of jealousy she felt at the sight of them together, and busied herself with helping to clear away. She shut her ears to the arrangements, privately deciding to sleep all next day if Jo spent it with John.

'I thought, Hester,' said John, raising his voice above the sound of clashing crockery, 'that you and Alicia might like to have lunch with Jo and me, as it's a special sort of day.'

Hester's eyes slid away from the challenge in John's, and she nodded.

'Very well. Thank you. How about you, Mother?'

Alicia turned from the washing up with a warm smile for John.

'Lovely. Thank you.'

He stood up carefully, Jo heavy with sleep against his shoulder.

'Good. I'll call for you at eleven-thirty. And now I think I'd better transport this young lady upstairs, and then I'll be off.'

There was an atmosphere of constraint as Hester followed John up to Jo's bedroom. He laid down his burden gently, and they both stood in silence, watching as their daughter wriggled herself into a position of comfort and snuggled down to sleep. Not a word was exchanged as they left the room and returned to the kitchen.

'Goodbye for the moment,' said John, smiling at Alicia. 'Thank you for a superb lunch. I'll look forward to returning the compliment tomorrow.'

'So shall I—look forward to it, I mean.' Alicia smiled, then turned away, aware that Hester was regarding them both with something very like resentment.

John gave Hester a brisk, impersonal smile.

'I'll see myself out. Why not have a rest too? You look shattered.'

'Which means I look like a hag,' she retorted.

'No. Dark circles under your eyes, that's all—nothing a good sleep won't put right.' John picked up his jacket, and with a casual wave left the two women together.

As the outer door closed Hester turned to her mother questioningly.

'You really like John a lot, don't you?'

'And you feel I shouldn't,' stated Alicia. 'You think I'm being disloyal.'

'No, not exactly——'

'But as he was responsible for your pregnancy you naturally feel I should harbour a grudge against him.'

Hester looked at Alicia ruefully, and sat down again at the table.

'Put in words like that it sounds a bit melodramatic, but roughly speaking I suppose that's what I do feel.'

Alicia came and sat down opposite.

'At first I did, naturally.' She looked very directly at Hester, her blue eyes candid. 'But you must admit that John moved heaven and earth to make amends, darling. He could just have made some financial settlement, paid his way out of the problem, but he didn't.'

'You mean he made an honest woman of me,' said Hester in a low voice.

'Not only that, Hester! He did his best to smooth the path for you in every possible way he could. Besides, I just took to him from the first. I was very sorry when you insisted on the divorce.'

Hester sat staring at her mother.

'Not quite in the usual line of mothers-in-law, are you, Mrs Price?'

Alicia laughed and got up to fill the kettle.

'Perhaps I would have been under normal circumstances.'

Hester's mouth drooped.

'As I said earlier, you obviously thought I should have stayed married to John.'

'It's what I would have done, in your place. But it's what you wanted that mattered, darling. Now let's have a cup of tea, shall we, and decide how to spend the rest of the afternoon when Jo wakes up.'

All three of them went shopping later on, enjoying some sudden winter sunshine while they found a hairdresser to tidy up Jo's hair. Hester, rather ashamed of her little outburst, treated her mother to a new blouse, and bought Jo some rather trendy dungarees and leather boots, finally standing them both to tea in a smart tea-shop to round off the afternoon.

'You're in spendthrift mood today,' observed Alicia, smiling. 'My blouse is beautiful, but I'd enjoy wearing it much more if you bought something for yourself, something you could wear tomorrow.'

'It isn't a special occasion—why should I need something new?' Hester busied herself with pouring more tea and wiping cream away from Jo's mouth.

'And how many times do you get asked out to lunch, may I ask?' Alicia asked caustically. 'When do you ever go out at all, in fact?'

'I don't care for socialising,' said Hester flatly, mindful of Jo's bright, interested eyes. 'But if it will make you happier I'll buy myself something new, if only a pair of tights.'

'Then you'd better get a move on,' advised her mother. 'Jo and I will finish our tea at leisure, then we'll go back to the car and listen to the radio. Off you go.'

Jo apparently quite happy with this arrangement, Hester went off at speed, finding it rather pleasant to look round the rapidly emptying shops on her own. She had nothing particular in mind, but admitted to herself that lunch with John, wherever he took them, put her on her mettle to look her best. She caught sight of herself in a mirror in the smart department store and stood still, utterly dismayed by her reflection. The night had definitely taken its toll, and she looked frankly awful. Her hair was escaping from its hastily wound knot, her face was bare of makeup, and her anorak and jeans were hardly the last word in elegance. Hester turned away in distaste, and made for the lift going up to the floor which displayed the more exclusive items.

Less than an hour later she arrived back at the car, breathless and apologetic, to find Jo consuming sweets out of a bag as she chatted to her grandmother and systematically coloured the book bought that afternoon.

'There was no need to rush, darling.' Alicia surveyed her daughter's flushed face with disapproval. 'You look as though you've run yourself ragged. Did you find something you liked?'

Hester dumped her parcels in the back with Jo, nodding.

'It's astonishingly easy if one's prepared to be extravagant. Not that I think "prepared" is quite the right word—but "extravagant" certainly is.'

'What did you buy, Mummy?' Jo was examining the elegant dress bags with interest.

'A skirt and a shirt, a belt and some boots, I'm afraid.' Hester grinned at Alicia as she backed the Mini-Traveller carefully out of the parking space. 'Once I'd started I couldn't stop!'

Alicia laughed.

'It seems to have done you good, anyway. Your cheeks are quite pink.'

'Sheer guilt! It all seemed like a good idea at the time, but I feel a bit conscience-stricken now the glow's fading.' Hester looked a little sheepish. 'I just couldn't resist buying a sort of shawl thing as well—God knows when I shall ever wear it!'

'You can wear it tomorrow when we go out with Daddy,' said Jo helpfully, looking at her grandmother with surprise as Alicia laughed and gave her a kiss.

CHAPTER FIVE

IT was cold and bright next day when John's Daimler drew up outside the house in Orchard Crescent. Jo had been in the bay window of the sitting room for at least half an hour, and jumped up and down in excitement, shouting that her Daddy had arrived as she ran to the front door. Alicia opened the door to John, but Jo brushed her aside, forgetting her manners in the heat of the moment.

'Daddy look—new boots!' She stood on one leg with the other in the air to display her new red footgear, almost toppling over in her enthusiasm. John scooped her up, presenting Alicia with the flowers he carried as he duly admired the boots, the dungarees and Jo's hair, which now it was properly trimmed looked rather endearing above her shining eyes and gamine grin.

'Is Mummy ready?' he asked, setting her down again.

'She'll be down in a moment,' said Alicia, and led the way into the sitting-room. 'I'm not coming with you today, John, though I appreciate very much being asked.'

John looked down at her searchingly.

'Aren't you well, Alicia?'

'I'm just fine, thanks, but I thought it might be a good idea if the three of you went out on your own. I'm having lunch with Barbara Drayton, and then we're going to the cinema, which is quite a treat on a Sunday.' Alicia smiled at him conspiratorially, and John bent and kissed her cheek.

'Have a nice day, as our American friends say.'

'Thank you. I'm sure I will. Now I must put these exquisite flowers in water, and Jo, run upstairs and hurry your mother up.'

Jo ran off happily and clattered up the stairs, shouting impatiently for her mother, while her father strolled over to the window and stared into the street.

Hester was ready when Jo came bursting into her room. She had been for the past few minutes, but some kind of paralysis seemed to have set in at the sound of the doorbell.

'Come *on*, Mummy——' Jo stopped as she saw Hester's outfit. 'Ooh—you look *lovely*!'

'Do you like it?' Hester glanced doubtfully in the mirror, but Jo tugged at her hand, and she followed the excited little figure downstairs, wishing she didn't feel so blatantly brand new. Nevertheless she was rather pleased with the full skirt in misty green wool, the loose shirt worn over it and cinched in at the waist with a wide tan belt that echoed the colour of her soft leather boots. The finishing touch, a great sweep of gold and green mohair had one end tucked into the belt and the other thrown over Hester's shoulder in a dramatic fringed swathe. To complement her expensive elegance Hester had coiled her hair tightly on the nape of her neck, and used rather more make-up than usual. The effect had seemed rather gratifying upstairs, but as she passed the hall mirror she felt suddenly overdressed and ridiculous. The look of startled admiration in John's eyes as he turned to greet her reassured Hester at once, and she smiled coolly, bidding him good morning with a casual poise meant to convey that jaunts of this kind were an everyday occurrence.

'You look extremely elegant,' John said. His eyes scrutinised her at leisure, taking in every detail from head to toe.

'Thank you. So do you,' she countered, which was the truth, even though John wore nothing more spectacular than a grey tweed suit and fine wool shirt. It was the negligent grace with which he wore them that made the difference, and which had never failed to raise her hackles in the past. Determined to avoid hostilities at all cost, Hester reminded herself that the day out was a treat for Jo, not for herself. Alicia's decision to stay behind had come as something of a shock the night before, but realising she was adamant Hester had resigned herself to the new arrangement with as good grace as possible, pleased that she had the new outfit to help shore up her confidence.

Once in the big, comfortable car, with Jo chattering nineteen to the dozen in the back seat, Hester began to relax. She glanced at John's profile as they left the built up area behind and drove through open country.

'Where are you taking us?' she asked idly.

'Home.'

Hester was startled. Jo often spent her day with her father at his house near Burford, as she knew very well. The child occasionally mentioned 'Daddy's house' in general terms, but Hester never asked questions, and during her visits to Camilla John was never discussed, as though his relationship to both women was a subject to be avoided at all costs.

'I thought you were taking us to a restaurant,' she said quietly.

'Did you?' After a swift look at her shuttered face John said no more. For the rest of the time the conversation was monopolised by Jo, who was happily exuberant to be going to 'Daddy's house' with both her parents, a situation new in her young life.

When the car finally turned into a long driveway, Hester felt keen anticipation despite herself. She expected to see an old house in typical Cotswold style with pointed gables and pitched roof, but the actuality was so far from her preconceived idea she stared blankly at what looked like a long, low, one-storey building, constructed of the beautiful local stone, admittedly, but with only a series of surprisingly small windows giving on to the drive, bisected by a huge modern door of heavy oak with smoked glass insets. The entire building was flanked by trees and hedges that masked the rest of the garden from view.

John leaned over to undo her seat belt, then got out to release his daughter. Hester opened the car door and emerged with eyes still fixed on the modernity of the house, which was so totally different from her imaginings.

'Come on, Mummy.' Jo tugged at her hand and pulled Hester towards the massive door that John unlocked to usher her through. He threw it open with what was rather a theatrical flourish for him, while Jo went dashing off through one of the doors leading from the large, square hall.

'Welcome to Prospect, Hester.' He led her across the gleaming, uncarpeted floor of the hall into a vast room where one wall was constructed entirely of glass. Too immense to be called a window, it gave a panoramic, breathtaking view of steeply shelving, rolling Cotswold countryside, and at first glance seemed to bring the outdoors into the very room itself, the effect intensified by the muted earth colours of the furnishings against plain cream walls and carpet. A stone fireplace held a log fire which John stooped to replenish as Hester stood in silence in the big, uncluttered room, lost for words. She was glad when Jo came in, followed by a little rough-haired dog with bright, intelligent eyes.

'Look, Mummy! *This* is Scrap. I told you about her.'

Hester had heard about Scrap at length, far more than any other feature of the days Jo spent with her father. She bent to pat the little black and white animal, laughing as the dog raised a front paw expectantly. She shook it, and straightened to smile at John.

'What breed would you say Scrap is?'

He chuckled and went down on his haunches to tickle the dog, who rolled over in ecstasy at the touch of the long fingers. 'Just a cross, I'm afraid.'

'She's not cross,' said Jo indignantly, patting Scrap consolingly.

'I didn't mean her temper, Jo. A cross means her— her daddy was a sheep dog and her mummy was a terrier.' John looked at Hester with a glint in his light eyes. 'And I fancy there may have been a few variations on a theme besides.'

Hester loosened the heavy wool shawl and John took it from her shoulders, laying it on the back of one of the suede couches flanking the fireplace. She strolled towards the window, smiling at Jo and the dog playing together on the carpet.

'She's a darling little dog,' she said casually over her shoulder, 'but I'd have pictured you with a wolf-hound or a Great Dane, something impressive to go with the house.'

'Do you like Daddy's house, Mummy?' asked Jo eagerly.

'It's lovely, darling. Breathtaking, in fact—I've never seen such a view.' Hester laughed a little as she turned towards John. 'Definitely not a room for agoraphobics!'

'Are you agoraphobic, Hester?'

'No.' She looked away from the unwavering, ice-grey eyes, to find Jo tugging at her hand, pulling her towards the door. 'What is it, darling?'

'Come and see Denny, she's ready to go!'

'Mrs Denham, my housekeeper,' explained John.

'Oh, I see.' Unwillingly Hester allowed herself to be guided across the hall to the kitchen, which was another eye-opener, fitted with every space age appliance for cooking any woman could ever want. An elderly, plump lady was ready to leave, already dressed in coat and hat, her rosy face alight with interest as Hester smiled at her rather shyly. Before she could say anything John announced, with deliberate emphasis, 'This is my wife, Denny.' Hester kept her smile straight with an effort.

'I'm very pleased to meet you,' said the housekeeper, smiling as she patted Jo on the head. 'Though I'm sure I feel I know you already, Mrs Ransome. This young lady talks about you all the time.'

'Oh dear,' said Hester faintly. 'That sounds ominous.'

Mrs Denham laughed comfortably.

'I hear you're an expert cook, so I do hope the lunch I've left will be to your taste. It's only cold, of course, though there's some soup in that pan there when you're ready, and jacket potatoes in the oven keeping hot. Mr Ransome said you'd serve yourselves.'

'Of course, Mrs Denham. I'm sure it will be delicious.' Hester smiled warmly, and the other woman took her leave, eager to be away.

The dining room was relatively small, with a lot less window, but still very spacious, with furniture made in Broadway and exquisitely plain cutlery crafted in Chipping Campden. Jo took Hester on a tour of the cold dishes laid out on the sideboard, much impressed with the big ham in pride of place among various salads and a wooden platter full of cheeses.

'It all looks gorgeous, Jo,' said Hester. 'But it's quite early. Unless you're actually starving can you hang on a bit before we eat?'

''Course I can,' said Jo and ran off to find Scrap who was waiting, panting, in the hall. 'Can I play in the garden, Daddy?'

'Put your duffel coat on first—the wind's chilly. You'll find a ball out there you can throw for Scrap.' John fastened Jo's coat and slid back a section of the living-room window for her to chase the barking dog outside down the flight of steps descending from the terrace to the steeply sloping lawn and the level area further down near the trees. Hester would have liked to go too, but John shut the window again before she could suggest it.

'Would you like to see the rest of the house?' he asked, 'or would you prefer a drink?'

'I've been wondering where the rest of the house actually is,' she said.

'The stairs lead down from the other end of the hall—you probably didn't notice as you came in. The rest of the rooms are on the floor below.'

Keeping on the move seemed preferable to just sitting, and with a look through the window to check on Jo, Hester followed John out of the room and down an open-tread spiral staircase. There were four bedrooms below, each of them furnished with restrained luxury, the largest and plainest obviously John's. Each room had its own bathroom to match the furnishings, and Hester was impressed.

'Jo said your house was big,' she commented, 'but I didn't realise it was on quite such a large scale. She's always been more forthcoming about the dog than anything else.'

'And of course you never asked.' John shut his bedroom door and leaned against it, arms folded.

'No, I didn't.' Hester eyed him uneasily. This was how she remembered him at their first meeting—or rather the second, she amended with bitterness. He was getting in her way again, as he had done either in person, or from a distance, for the past six years.

John waved a hand towards the stair well. 'Let's have that drink now, shall we?'

Hester inclined her head and mounted the stairs, her back straight as she preceded John into the beautiful living room and went over to the window to make sure Jo was all right. She hoped this terrible feeling of insecurity would fade in time, but at the moment it was an effort to leave Jo for a second without a sensation of panic. Jo was running and laughing with the eager Scrap down in the garden, and Hester seated herself on one of the couches, where she could watch Jo in comfort. John strolled over to a cabinet at the far side of the room.

'What would you like, Hester?'

She glanced over at him, shrugging.

'I don't know. We only ever have sherry at home. The whisky you drank was a prize Mother won at her bridge club raffle.' She got up and went over to inspect the contents of the cabinet, which appeared to hold everything drinkable she'd ever heard of, and quite a few she hadn't. 'What do you suggest?'

John's mouth curved in a challenging smile.

'How about a Bourbon Old-fashioned? I developed quite a taste for them in the States.'

Hester had no intention of admitting her ignorance, and rashly said 'Why not? I'd love one.'

There was an annoyingly indulgent look on John's face as he mixed the drink and handed her the glass. Hester took it gingerly and took a mouthful. Only cast iron self control stopped her from choking as the strong smoky flavour of the spirit hit her, unadulterated by anything other than sugar and a dash of Angostura bitters. She returned to the couch quickly to get her breath back. If John noticed he said nothing, merely following her to lean against the stone chimney breast, sipping his own drink, his eyes on Jo in the garden.

'She won't be cold, do you think Hester?'

'Not while she's on the move. She'll be hungry in a minute—perhaps I ought to see to the soup——'

'Finish your drink,' he interrupted. 'I'll see to the meal.'

Hester looked up at him curiously.

'I just can't see you in an apron, Jack.'

He smiled, his eyes mocking.

'How do you see me, then?'

'Oh, in formal clothes, being tremendously authoritative, telling people what to do and how to do it, I suppose.' She took another cautious swallow, not caring for the drink much, but glad of its relaxing effect.

'I'm surprised, not to mention flattered, that you spare a thought for me at all,' he said with irony.

'I can hardly fail to with such a constant little reminder on hand all the time!' Hester's response was more tart than she intended, and the sudden clenching of John's jaw made her feel a little remorseful. 'I didn't intend to snap, Jack. I seem to be developing into something of a shrew as I get older.'

'And that, no doubt, is something you also lay at my door,' he said bleakly, staring into the fire.

'No. I don't.' Hester drained her glass and put it down. 'My way of life is my own choice. So I can hardly complain when—when things get rough now and again. Generally I'm very much in control, with no hangups. But nothing could have prepared me for the shock of Jo's kidnap—even if it was a fiasco in the end. To be honest it was one occasion, at least, when I didn't relish being a single parent.'

'But you aren't a single parent in fact, Hester.' John's voice was steel-hard.

'No,' she agreed soberly. 'Only in practice.'

'Shall I tell you what really disturbs me?' he asked suddenly, straightening. He stood looking down at her, hands in pockets. Hester shook her head. 'I wonder what will happen when you marry again—have other children.'

She laughed shortly.

'Then you can stop troubling yourself. I don't intend to, ever.'

John turned away to add more logs to the flames, putting a fine mesh guard in front of the fire afterwards. As the logs caught the flames flickered red, washing colour into his lean face momentarily, giving his coldly chiselled features an unaccustomed heat.

'You are only twenty-seven, Hester. You should be living a normal, fulfilled life with a husband and other children, instead of immuring yourself in that austere little room or slaving your life away in a kitchen.' He spoke with a restrained violence that affected Hester deeply.

'But I *am* fulfilled Jack. I like cooking, and I don't lack for company. I have Mother and Jo and——'

'And what?' John put out a hand and grasped her wrist, pulling her to her feet, his face only inches from hers. 'Don't you ever feel even the faintest inclination towards masculine company? The need to go out with a man, talk to a man——'

'And go to bed with a man?' Hester's eyes clashed with his. 'I once had that pleasure granted to me, remember? I'm hardly likely to want the episode repeated, I assure you!'

There was a silence that set her teeth on edge, then John released her hand and Hester went over to the great window, knocking on the glass to attract Jo's attention. Her breathing slowed and she got hold of herself again as the child came toiling up the steps to the terrace outside, the faithful hound in tow.

'Do you allow them straight in from the garden on this beautiful carpet?' she asked.

'It's very dry, and I don't relish the prospect of parting Jo from her new boots. I'll deal with the dog.' John slid the window open and fielded Scrap as Jo came running in.

'Stay there on the terrace,' said Hester hastily. 'Let me see if your boots are dirty.'

Very unwillingly Jo allowed her mother to remove the new boots, and chattering like a magpie she danced into the hall in her socks, obediently going to wash her hands while Hester dusted off her boots and John put the soup to heat.

Jo's happy chatter was a boon during lunch. It lightened the atmosphere between her parents to the point where they could talk quite normally on safe, general topics, keeping off personalities while they did justice to Mrs Denham's excellent beef soup, and the beautifully prepared salads that followed it as an accompaniment to the succulent ham. John produced a smooth claret to drink with the meal and provided ice-cream for Jo's dessert, but sent a smile in Hester's direction as he pushed only the cheeseboard towards her.

'I thought you might be bored with sweet things. I told Denny not to bother, that you'd probably prefer cheese. Was I right?'

'Absolutely. Much as I enjoy concocting them I'm not really fond of puddings.'

'Does the hotel lay down any rules about what you cook?'

Hester helped herself to Stilton. 'Not really. Alain lets me do my own thing mainly, as long as I keep to categories. What I think of as a gooey, a fluffy, a creamy, a pie, cake and pudding.' She laughed at his expression. 'I ring the changes as often as possible, and some things are seasonal, of course.'

'And you really get pleasure from doing that all the time?' he asked.

'Yes. I do.' Hester glanced at Jo, who was lolling in her chair after demolishing a large bowlful of neapolitan ice-cream. 'Are you full, chicken?'

Jo nodded sleepily.

'Shall I go and have my rest now, Daddy?' she said, to Hester's surprise.

'Jo usually has forty winks on my bed when we have lunch here,' explained John. 'In company with Scrap, of course.'

'Good idea.' And what do we do, thought Hester. Resume hostilities once Jo's tucked up in bed, probably.

John had coffee ready in the living room when Hester went back upstairs after settling Jo down. He gestured for her to pour out.

'Shouldn't we wash up first?' she suggested.

'Definitely not. I've cleared the food away and put the dishes in the dish-washer. You can just sit there and look ornamental.' John took the cup she handed him and sat on the couch opposite, a slight smile on his face. If it was meant to put Hester at her ease it failed. She looked away, keeping her eyes on the garden as she sipped her coffee.

'It must be very beautiful here in summer,' she said, and smiled brightly at him. 'Jo said one day you had a lot of glass, but somehow I pictured a collection of crystal in cabinets, not windows.'

He lit a cigar and looked at her lazily through the smoke. 'I'm not really the bits and pieces type, Hester. Not quite so rigidly spartan as you, of course, but I don't like clutter, either.'

'No. I can see that.'

'Will you have a liqueur, or a brandy?'

Hoping the alcohol would help her to relax a little, Hester nodded. 'Yes, I would, please. A small glass of Benedictine, if you have it.'

John went over to the cabinet, shrugging off his jacket on the way. The fine cream wool of his shirt clung to his broad shoulders and slim waist, revealing a muscular shape his more formal attire normally concealed. Hester scrutinised his back view with detachment. He wore his hair slightly longer than she remembered, and if anything she fancied he was thinner than when they married. He turned with the drinks and caught her watching him.

'Something wrong?' he asked, and strolled over to sit beside her on the couch.

Hester took the glass he gave her and shook her head. There was something wrong, nevertheless. She disliked the unavoidable intimacy of the situation; the two of them alone in front of the fire in the fading light of the winter afternoon.

'I was just thinking you were thinner than you used to be,' she said truthfully.

'So are you, if that's possible.' John slid an arm along the back of the couch, not touching her, but too close for Hester's preference.

'I lead an active life,' she said colourlessly, and sipped her liqueur.

'So do I.'

'You must do, to have achieved so much so early in life.'

'I'm thirty-six, Hester. Hardly juvenile. And it all depends on what you mean by so much.' He swivelled slightly to look at her face. 'Forging ahead in the rat-race has been my compensation for those other things I lack—an attempt to fill the gap left by the absence of a home life.'

Hester gave him a wry, considering look, and gestured at the room.

'You have a beautiful home, Jack.'

'A house, Hester, not a home.' The satiric gleam was back in his eyes. 'I have no wife to give those feminine touches necessary to a home. I do have a beautiful child, certainly, but I see pitifully little of her.' He reached out and took the glass from her hand, putting it down on the coffee tray with care before taking her chin in his hand and turning her face towards him. 'Oddly enough I was less aware of the deficiencies in my life before Jo was old enough for me to see her regularly. These days I grow more and more reluctant to part with her every time I bring her back. She's so bright and intelligent and—and loving, I suppose describes her best. The odd circumstances of her life seem to leave her unaffected. No one would ever guess she was the child of a broken marriage.'

Hester pushed his hand away impatiently, disliking the touch of his fingers against her skin.

'The situation has been constant from her birth,' she said, and met his eyes head on, her own steady. 'And you can hardly use the word broken for a marriage that never got off the ground in the first place.'

'Only because you refused to let it!' He turned away, his face cold.

'However you choose to describe it, for Jo it's the norm——'

'It's not for me though,' he interrupted harshly. 'Nor can I believe it is for you. It's bloody unnatural. You, living like a nun, and me—well, not totally celibate, the nature of the beast being what it is, but the next best thing to it.'

'You can hardly blame me for your life-style—it's

nothing to do with me,' Hester snapped, glaring at him with dislike.

'That's where you're wrong. It's everything to do with you.' John's face took on an unaccustomed dark colour along his cheekbones as he took her hand and held it in an iron grip to keep her where she was, sensing her instinct for escape. 'Let me tell you a little story, my dear Hester, now that we have this entirely unexpected opportunity to be alone.'

'I don't want to hear it.' She struggled to free herself, but he held her fast, his eyes obdurate as he went on.

'Nevertheless I intend that you listen. So keep still and you won't be hurt. I want to go back to our first encounter.' John ignored Hester's instant recoil and continued in a quiet, less heated tone. 'When I found out what I'd done that next morning, or rather when Camilla went up like a rocket when she found me in the wrong bed. No,' as she tried vainly to pull away. 'No, Hester, let's bring it out in the open, talk about it with honesty. Camilla went on hysterically about "Miss Price who did the catering', with never a word about what you were like, or how young you were.'

'What difference did that make?' she demanded angrily.

He thrust his free hand through his hair impatiently. 'None, of course, in one way. But I genuinely thought the victim of my drunken indiscretion was some maiden lady of uncertain age who was likely to have me up in court at the very least. I came chasing out to see you, prepared to go down on bended knees, throw myself on your mercy—anything. I was in a muck sweat all the way in the car, and when your mother answered the door I thought *she* was Miss Price!'

An unwilling little laugh escaped Hester. 'I wish I'd known,' she said with malice. 'As it was, I just thought you felt ill.'

'Ill!' He shot her a mirthless grin. 'Those moments in your office while I waited for you were among the

longest and worst of my life. Not *the* worst. That was
still to come, but pretty high in the agony ratings just
the same. Then you came in and I was utterly
dumbfounded.'

Hester turned to look at him curiously.

'Why?'

'You had flour on your nose and your hair was short
then. You were wearing jeans and a striped butcher's
apron. Had you any idea of how young you looked?'
She shook her head, and he let out an explosive sigh.
'For a wild moment, Hester, I thought you were about
twelve, and my crime swung from one end of the scale
to the other. An offence against a minor this time. And
then you smiled and said something, and I really
plumbed the depths.'

'In what way?'

'Because if we'd met under any other circumstances
whatsoever I would have done my damndest to make
you like me. Asked you out to dinner——'

'But you did.' Hester looked down demurely.

'I remember only too well. I sent you flowers too.
What I'm trying to explain is that for me there was a
feeling of recognition when I saw you, as though we
had already met——'

'We had,' she pointed out cruelly.

'For God's sake, Hester——' John broke off and
dropped her hand, and for a moment she thought he
would jump to his feet and leave her. But he stayed.
And after a while went on, in control once more. 'I
don't know why I still react so violently. God knows I
should be used to your attitude. It was hardly likely to
be any different, even after all this time. You still feel
the same disgust, even now Hester.'

She was conscious of a surprising feeling of remorse.

'No, not disgust, Jack. That's too strong a word.
Resentment, perhaps——'

'You definitely felt disgust that day, even loathing,'
he said heavily.

'What did you expect?' she countered. 'I was hardly likely to fall on your neck and smother you with gratitude, was I?'

'No,' he said shortly, his face set. They were quiet for some time, both staring at the flames, neither of them aware of their surroundings as both of them remembered that first meeting.

'This—this recognition you say you felt,' said Hester at last. 'Was that part of the reason for marrying me when you knew I was pregnant? Would you have been so adamant if I was a bit more unprepossessing?'

'God knows,' said John wearily. 'I hope I would have done everything I could for anyone I'd injured in that way. With you marriage seemed the logical way to pay my debt. You know, for a while there afterwards in the hospital I really thought you were coming round to the idea of being my wife. I sensed a definite warmth.'

Hester turned away, her eyes shuttered.

'Only the merest flicker, Jack. It died a sudden death when I heard you were living with another woman at the same time.'

'I was not living with Laura,' he said tightly. 'I explained all that at the time. She worked for me, and at one time we occasionally slept together. But from the moment I met you all that side of it was over.'

'Does she still work for you?'

'No. She's married. Does it make any difference?' He eyed her sardonically.

'None.'

'I thought you might like to know who'd replaced her.'

Hester turned a cold stare on his mocking face.

'Why should I?'

He shrugged. 'Why you do, or think, anything has always been a mystery to me, Hester. I thought you might like the records straight. My new assistant goes by the name of Harrison, not long out of college, receding hair and wears glasses. Perhaps you heard me mention him the night Jo was missing.'

Hester flushed, smarting under his sarcasm, and took refuge in the remaining contents of her liqueur glass, leaning forward deliberately to take it from the tray, and replacing it afterwards with finicking care. She avoided the ice-grey eyes she knew were unwavering on her face, and sat quietly, her hands folded in her lap, hoping Jo would wake up and interrupt this uncomfortable tête-à-tête. The house was very quiet, only the crackle of the fire relieving the tense silence in the vast, beautiful room. It was a relief when John began to speak again, his voice carefully casual.

'Unlike your blameless existence, Hester, I do occasionally take some attractive woman out to dine, or the theatre, maybe even to a nightclub, when I'm in London. I have a flat in Chelsea—did you know?'

'No,' she answered shortly.

'Sometimes I even spend the night with the lady, whoever she is, if she's agreeable.' John laughed a little, leaning to look into her unwilling eyes. 'But of course you've never given a thought to my activities all these years, have you, Hester? You've never felt a moment's curiosity about what I do, or who I do it with.'

'No, I'm afraid I haven't,' she said composedly. Which was a downright lie. Often and often she had longed to know how he was, or if he intended marrying again, if he were back with Laura or had someone else. But thumbscrews would never have made her admit it. Even to herself she never acknowledged that half her eagerness to visit Camilla was the hope of hearing something about John. But she could never bring herself to ask, and Camilla obviously thought it best never to mention his name.

'I have never brought anyone here, by the way,' he said casually. 'The only feminine footsteps here are Denny's, Jo's and Camilla's—unless you count Scrap.'

Hester shifted a little in her seat, wishing he would move away.

'I've no idea why you're telling me all this. It's nothing to do with me.'

'Then why are you so uneasy?' He moved closer and captured her hand again. 'Your pulse is racing. What's the matter?'

She turned to face him, her brows drawn together over suspicious green eyes.

'*You*'re the matter, Jack. It's you that's making me nervous. I'd never have agreed to come today if I'd thought that . . .' she trailed away, her mouth drying at the caressing look in his eyes.

'If you'd thought that I'd bring you home and make you spend the afternoon alone with me,' he said helpfully. 'Is that what's causing all the trouble, Hester? The thought that no one lives for miles around, and our only company is our child sleeping downstairs.'

She tried to move away, rattled by the emphasis he put on the word 'our'. John's hand held her still as his other arm descended on her shoulders and she was trapped. Alarm signals went off inside her head and she sat ramrod stiff, waiting for his next move, prepared to spring to her feet and run at the slightest relaxation of his hold.

'No, Hester,' he said pleasantly. 'I'm not going to let you go.'

'Please, Jack!' She gave him a hunted look. 'It's time I woke Jo—we should be going home——'

'You *are* home. And I think we should let Jo sleep.' John drew nearer, his eyes intent on her flushed, wary face. 'I'm not going to attack you, Hester. Perhaps if I make my intentions clear you'll feel less nervous. I have this irrepressible urge to kiss you just once again. Not like the other night, when you were like a dead thing, and I was acting under impulse. Here and now I have a real, live woman in my arms—don't bother to contradict, I can feel your pulse, your warmth.' He pulled her close, tightening his arm round her waist while the other hand turned her face up to his. 'Don't bother to deny it, Hester. There are responses in that lovely body of yours, I know, and just this once, while I have the opportunity, I intend to prove it once and for all.'

'No, Jack, please——'

'Yes, Hester, *please*!' His answer was a mocking parody of her plea, and she twisted under his hands, provoking exactly the opposite response from the one she sought. His mouth came down on hers and her pleading was stifled, and to her shame this time she found it quite impossible to stay limp and lifeless in his arms. The first touch of his lips seemed to be the signal for a multiplicity of sensation that flamed through her entire body, and without any power to prevent it her mouth opened and allowed his tongue to caress and twine with hers, taking her breath away and rendering her helpless to oppose the hands that caressed and smoothed her body until it shaped to his as faithfully as though it had been made for just this purpose.

'You see,' he muttered against her mouth. 'You do respond. You can come to life——'

'Can I come in?' said an aggrieved voice from the doorway, and Hester tore herself out of John's arms and ran to hold Jo close, glad the room was too dimly lit for her child's sharp eyes to see the colour flaming in her mother's face.

'Sorry, darling,' she said breathlessly, 'we thought you were sleep. Have you washed your face?'

Jo nodded, and looked at her father accusingly as she scampered towards him.

'I went back to the bathroom when I saw you kissing Mummy,' she said, frowning. 'And when I came back you were *still* kissing Mummy.'

Hester felt agonisingly embarrassed, but John merely picked up his scolding daughter and settled her on his lap, grinning at her.

'I like kissing Mummy,' he said impenitently, and gave her a smacking kiss on her warm, flushed cheek. 'I like kissing you, too. Where's Scrap.'

'I let her out. She wanted walkies.'

'I expect she did!' John ruffled the short hair. 'Are you thirsty?'

'Yes.'

'What would you like? Orange juice, coke——'

Jo shuddered and burrowed her face against him.

'Don't like coke any more.'

John hugged her close.

'No, darling, I don't suppose you do. Perhaps Mummy will get a glass of juice for you.' He looked up at Hester. 'Would you mind organising us some tea? You'll find everything necessary in the kitchen.'

'No. I'd be glad to.' Which was the literal truth. Hester left the room thankfully and pressed light switches in the hall and kitchen, glad to escape from John for the moment. She winced at the bright clinical strip-lighting as she filled a kettle and plugged it in. While it boiled she tidied herself up in the cloakroom, replaiting and coiling her hair tightly, putting lipstick on her pink, swollen mouth. She frowned at her reflection in distaste, flushing when she saw her shirt was undone. She did it up hurriedly, her mouth compressed as she made the necessary repairs. She must have been out of her mind to let John make love to her like that. Only she hadn't just let him. She had joined in with quite reprehensible abandon, and there was little point in deluding herself she had just suffered his mouth and hands. She had enjoyed their touch so thoroughly it had taken Jo's appearance to put a stop to it all.

Mrs Denham had left a tea-tray ready in the kitchen, complete with a container of home made biscuits ready to decant on to the silver basket waiting with the cups and saucers. Hester made tea in the wicker-handled pottery tea-pot, found a carton of juice in the refrigerator, and poured some into a glass for Jo, then carried the tray into the living room. John took it from her in silence, with a wry look at her ruthlessly tidy hair, and put the tray on the table in front of the sofa where the cushions were now smooth, all traces of those heated few minutes removed.

Jo was in good form for a while after her nap, fortunately, entertaining her somewhat preoccupied parents with anecdotes from school while she fed Scrap bits of her biscuit. Hester sat listening absently until Jo said something which turned her cold.

'The man won't come for me again, will he, Daddy?'

John's eyes met Hester's, arrested.

'No, sweetheart, of course he won't,' he said reassuringly.

'I'll fetch you every day, in any case, Jo,' added Hester quickly.

'But if you can't come again one day, will *he* come?' Jo persisted, her face very anxious.

'I shan't ever go away again, Jo. I promise!' Hester looked over at John in anguished appeal. 'And even if I have to I'll just tell Daddy, and he'll come.'

'But the man said it was Daddy, and it wasn't.' Jo's lips drooped and she put her thumb in her mouth.

This upset Hester more than anything else. Jo had given up thumb-sucking from eighteen months on, and it was very disturbing to see her revert to the babyhood habit. They had taken her resilience too much for granted, that was obvious, and the kidnapping had affected her more deeply than they thought. John went down on one knee beside Jo and put a finger under her chin, turning the troubled little face up to his.

'It won't happen again, Jo, I promise you. The police will catch the man and then he won't be able to steal little girls away ever again.'

'Will they hurt him, Daddy?'

'No. But they'll put him in prison.'

'Not the lady, please.' Jo's eyes filled with tears. 'I *liked* the lady.'

John gathered her up in his arms and cradled her

against him as she began to cry in earnest, sobbing into his shirt in heart-wrenching misery. Hester had to struggle against tears herself.

'Darling, please,' she begged. 'Don't cry like that. You'll make yourself ill.'

'I'm frightened, Mummy,' sobbed Jo. 'I don't want—to go—home.'

'But Jo, don't you want to see Grandma and sleep in your own bed?'

The child shook her head violently, and clung harder to her father.

'Want to stay here.'

John looked at Hester over the cropped little head.

'Perhaps just for tonight?' he suggested quietly. 'This is a bit of delayed reaction, I think. She'll be fine tomorrow.'

'But I have to get back——' began Hester, then stopped abruptly at the look he gave her.

'Why?' he asked coldly. 'Which is more important—your daughter or that job of yours?'

'*Pas devant mon enfant*,' snapped Hester, emphasizing the possessive pronoun. Jo had no experience of parental squabbles and her mother had no intention of adding to her distress, so she said reasonably, 'Let's wait a little while. See how things are later.'

Hester and John were very matter of fact with each other after that, in an effort to calm Jo down, both of them shaken by the sight of the usually sunny Jo reduced to this pathetic, tear-sodden little creature who refused to be detached from the security of her father's strong arms. Eventually Hester left them together and washed the tea things to give herself breathing space, and an opportunity to think. She was unlikely to lose her concession for desserts from the hotel, she knew. Alain Girardin, the manager, was a kind, understanding man who took a personal interest in the people who worked for him, and would be very sympathetic under the circumstances. Alicia was more than likely to be highly delighted that Hester and John were sleeping under the same roof, so it seemed best to give in with good grace for just the one night. By the next day Jo would no doubt be her normal, bubbling self again, and certainly no one would think it strange if she missed school for a day after her ordeal.

Hester went back to the living room with a smile for Jo, who was watching a children's television serial from the safety of her father's lap. John raised an eyebrow.

'Well?' he asked.

'All right. We'll stay—but just for tonight.'

His face softened, and Jo jumped off his knee and ran to Hester, hugging her in an ecstasy of gratitude. She turned an anxious, red-eyed face up to her mother.

'Will Grandma be sad on her own?'

'Oh no, not for one night. I'll ring her when she comes home from the cinema, and she'll understand. Now sit quietly for a bit and watch the serial; all that crying has worn you out.' Hester stooped to kiss the blotchy little cheek. 'Oh look, Jo, poor Scrap is very worried—she doesn't like to see you cry.'

Jo immediately got down on the carpet in front of the fire to make a fuss of Scrap, then lay on her stomach with her arm across the little dog to watch the rest of the programme. John sat with her for a while, then got up to draw the heavy silk curtains across the great window, motioning Hester to follow him out of the room to a door at the far side of the hall, near the head of the stairs. It was his study, very functional and well-designed, with filing cabinets and computer and walls lined with bookshelves. He closed the door behind them and sat on the edge of the desk.

'You look shattered, Hester,' he said, examining her face.

'I feel shattered. It tears me apart to see Jo cry like that. She's never been a howling sort of child.' Hester shook her head, shuddering. 'I feel so guilty, Jack. I realise I should have expected all this, but she went off so happily last night and slept through the night. She was really exhausted, I suppose, but she made no objections when I put her to bed.'

John's face was sombre.

'But now she's had time to think it all out, Hester. Somewhere along the line it's dawned on her that they know where she lives, and where she goes to school. It's taken a day to sink in. The fact that they really meant to take the Rantzen child doesn't mean a thing to Jo, because she herself was the one they actually made off with.'

'Yes, you're right,' she agreed, and sighed. 'She feels safe here because she thinks they can't find her. Well, we'll see how she is after staying the night. Perhaps it will restore her sense of security.'

John looked at her questioningly.

'And if it doesn't?'

'We'll meet that when we come to it.' Hester looked away. 'In the meantime you go back to Jo, and I'll see if Mother's back from her day out. May I use the 'phone?' she added.

He went over to the door, giving her a mocking little smile.

'You may do anything you wish here, Hester. As they say in Spain, "my house is yours".'

CHAPTER SIX

AFTER explaining the situation to Alicia, who was all for Hester and Jo staying where they were, as anticipated, Hester tried to make the best of things for the rest of the evening and devoted her full attention to Jo until it was time to put her to bed. John brought out a pack of cards and the three of them played a modified form of Snap, allowing Jo to win most of the time, to her triumph. Afterwards she took a great deal of coaxing before she would eat any supper, even when allowed to picnic from a tray in front of the fire, and this added further to Hester's disquiet, as normally Jo's appetite remained constant through thick and thin. As bedtime approached Hester became more and more worried. In her present frame of mind it seemed probable Jo would protest violently against being left alone for the night, but after a lively bath presided over by her father, and gales of laughter when he produced a large white sweatshirt of his own for her to sleep in, she settled down in the smallest of the bedrooms quite contentedly, due to John's brainwave. He moved Scrap's basket into the room, and with the little dog on the floor beside her, and a small lamp left alight on the bedside table, Jo snuggled down to sleep without a murmur.

'Thank God for Scrap,' said Hester. She felt utterly limp by the time they returned to the living room. 'And I don't mean for my sake, but for Jo's. She was perfectly happy with the dog for company.'

John kicked a log into the flames angrily.

'I'd like to get my hands on the bastard who made her like this. "Saviours of the Earth", be damned. I'd ram his teeth down his throat by way of openers——'

'I know how you feel,' said Hester hastily, 'but it doesn't do any good, Jack. She'll probably be right as rain tomorrow.'

'You think so?' He turned on her morosely. 'It will suit you very well if she is, of course. I'm sure you can't wait to get out from under my roof and turn tail for the cloisters, but this time it's Jo we're putting first, my darling ex-wife, not you.'

'That's not fair! I always put Jo first—my entire life is spent in thinking of Jo first and myself second.' Hester was stung by his injustice.

'And I come last! If you ever spare a thought for me at all.' John swung away to stare blackly into the fire.

'As your part in Jo's presence on earth was somewhat minimal, what else do you expect?'

'I'm not referring to myself as Jo's father, for God's sake, but as a man with an entity of my own. Can't you ever think of me as plain John Ransome?'

They stared at each other malevolently, their argument no less bitter for being conducted in an undertone, to avoid disturbing Jo.

'It has never been my habit to think of you in any capacity at all!' Hester turned sharply and sat down on the couch, staring down at her tightly clenched hands in her lap, angry with John, herself, the whole world at that particular moment. There was an uneasy silence while she faced the fact that her anger was caused more by present shortcomings than past. It caught her on the raw to feel that John was apparently able to shrug off their earlier lovemaking as casually as if it had been a game of chess. But then, that sort of thing was a commonplace occurrence for him, no doubt. For her it was different. The silence became unbearable, Hester burningly aware that John's eyes were fixed on her downbent head. 'I shouldn't have been so cutting,' she said at last, without looking up. 'I was knocked sideways by Jo's outburst, but that last remark was uncalled for. I'm sorry.'

John moved to her side and laid a hand on her shoulder.

'I was no better, Hester. It's been bloody awful for all of us, and I suppose it was only natural to hit out at each other.' He smiled as she looked up at him ruefully, his eyes softening as they noted the dark rings under hers. 'Why don't you go downstairs and have a rest, Hester. The beds are made up in all the rooms.'

Hester got up and smiled, accepting the olive branch. 'What I'd really like, Jack, is a bath. Would you mind?'

'God no, help yourself.' He relaxed visibly. 'Take your time, have a nice long soak. I'll rustle up something to eat in the meantime.'

'I should be doing that,' said Hester doubtfully. 'Can you manage?'

'I'm not entirely helpless in the kitchen, I'll have you know,' he said lightly. 'I always see to myself on Sundays anyway. Denny only came in today because this was a special occasion. Go on. Half an hour and no longer. We'll have a picnic in front of the fire when you're ready.'

A hot bath was always Hester's remedy for tension, and she sighed with relief as she lay full length in a tub of perfumed water, her hair wrapped in a towel to protect it from the steam. The fresh scent came from the tall flask of bath oil, and gave off a sharp, citrus fragrance that Hester liked. She approved John's taste in decoration, too, as she lay gazing round the room, wondering if he had chosen the colours himself or called in professionals to do it for him. She liked the effect of white louvred cupboards and primrose yellow tub, the walls a riot of spring flowers on a background of pale green. Feathery green ferns in a white ceramic pot stood on a wicker shelf which also held a pile of thick, fluffy towels, and Hester sighed, reluctant to get out of the bath. It was definitely a place to linger.

When she was dressed again Hester had to leave her hair loose, the steam having tightened the curl so much it was impossible to plait. She added a touch of lipstick then went to take a look at Jo, who was sleeping soundly, her small canine guard in attendance. Feeling reassured and more relaxed, Hester ran up the polished wood staircase in her stockinged feet, boots in hand, almost colliding with John as he came out of the study.

'I was just coming to hurry you up—I've put the coffee on. I thought perhaps you'd dozed off in the bath.' He grinned and put out a hand to touch her hair. 'Couldn't manage to flatten it down this time?'

'No. I had the bathwater a bit hot.' Hester indicated her boots. 'Do you mind if I leave these off? They're new, and my feet are protesting a bit.'

John shrugged, giving her a somewhat indulgent look as he followed her to one of the couches. He drew up a small table in front of it and motioned her to sit down.

'As I said earlier, Hester, you can do exactly as you wish in this house.'

'Do you say that to all your visitors, Jack?'

'No. I don't. How was Jo?'

'Out for the count. Scrap, too.'

John laughed, obviously pleased his brainwave had worked, and went out to the kitchen to bring in a laden tray which he set down in front of Hester with an air of self-congratulation.

'There. Ham sandwiches and walnut cake, cheese and coffee. How did I do?'

'Full marks,' said Hester. 'Did you make mustard? Great.' She found she was suddenly hungry, despite the delicious lunch, and put her appetite down to an excess of emotion, one way and another.

'I didn't open any more wine. I thought you'd prefer a drink later,' said John.

'Just as well. I've already drunk as much today as I normally do in six months, anyway.'

John put down a sandwich half-eaten, and stared at her, shaking his head.

'Now don't rip at me, Hester, but don't you ever

have a yen for some different kind of existence? Are you genuinely content to pass your days just cooking and looking after Jo?' He leaned towards her, his eyes searching. 'What happens when she'd old enough to go out with friends, take off for college?'

'She'll just go. I shan't stand in her way.' Hester cut herself a slice of cake, unruffled. 'My mother never held me back in any way. It was sheer coincidence that I chose to work from home with my own business, not any idea of hers. And if Jo in turn wants to be a nuclear-scientist or a movie-star, I'll encourage her all I can. Don't worry, Jack, I shan't be a possessive mother, trying to hang on to her, I promise.'

John resumed eating, his thoughtful eyes on the flames.

'You know, Hester, at first I thought I'd never be able to exist under the load of guilt weighing me down when I first married you. I used to visit you in that hospital room and feel like a criminal just to know that you were there in such a rotten state of health purely as a direct result of my own actions, however unintentional.'

Hester looked at him curiously.

'Is that why you insisted on visiting me? Guilty conscience?'

'Partly,' he admitted. 'I used to talk to your mother quite a lot about you——'

'Really?' Hester stared at him in surprise. 'When?'

John looked slightly uncomfortable.

'Sometimes after visiting you at the hospital. I used to feel like such an out and out heel—well, I just needed some comfort, odd though it may seem. There was none at all from Camilla, which will hardly surprise you, and my parents were already living in Portugal by then, so I turned to Alicia. I hoped she would be compassionate. And she was.'

Hester was astonished. 'She's never mentioned it—don't tell me these secret sessions carried on after I left hospital!'

'No. Once you were adamant about divorce it hardly seemed ethical. Could I have some coffee, please?'

'What? Oh, yes, of course.' Hester busied herself with the cups, frowning, trying to digest what John had told her. There were hidden depths in her mother's character. Surprising ones. She glanced at John curiously. 'What did you talk about during these illicit encounters?'

'You, mainly.' John took a cup from her and smiled with a wry twist of the lips. 'For a start I learned you'd hardly ever been ill in your life until I dawned on the scene. That made me feel great, as you can imagine. It made my visits to you even more difficult. I used to sit there in your hospital room, almost frying in the infra red waves of resentment coming from you, when all the time I knew that you were so ill solely because of me. Put yourself in my place, Hester. Just for once try to think of it from my angle.'

She gave an unexpected giggle.

'Are you a masochist, by any chance? I never wanted you there in the slightest, yet you insisted on turning up. You must have dreaded the weekends.'

'They mark them in red on church calendars,' he said sardonically. 'They were hardly red letter days for me.'

'Then why did you keep on coming?'

He shrugged.

'They got better gradually.' He glanced at the tray. 'All these revelations are making me hungry. Could I have that last sandwich?'

Hester passed the plate, still taken up with her mother's double life.

'It really amazes me that my mother could have kept your meetings to herself, though. Did you ask her not to tell me about the little heart-to-hearts?'

'No. That was her decision. She had an idea you might object.' He raised a sardonic eyebrow. 'And of course you would have.'

Hester nodded.

'I was in rather an emotional state, one way and another—hardly at my most rational. But I rather suspected Mother had a soft spot for you, Jack.'

He held out his cup for more coffee, his face sombre.

'A good thing someone does.'

'Oh come on, Jack Ransome! Your daughter thinks you're the greatest. And I do read the local newspaper now again. You sometimes get a mention with some lovely lady in tow. They can't all be wrong.'

'One has to pass the time somehow,' he said expressionlessly. 'And you can hardly count Jo. I'm the excitement in her life—the chap who collects her in a big car and takes her out for treats. I'm the jam, not the bread and butter.'

'And who was she clinging to today?' demanded Hester. 'Not me, you notice, but Daddy.'

John picked up the tray and stood looking down at her. 'Did you mind, Hester?'

'I felt a pang,' she said honestly. 'But I understood. I can see how her mind is working. To her this house is sanctuary. She feels safe here—with you.' She got to her feet. 'I'll wash up.'

'Unnecessary. I'm just going to dump these in the kitchen.' John moved to the door, but Hester followed him and laid a hand on his arm.

'You have a look at Jo. I'll wash up. Please.'

John halted, the muscles of his arm tense beneath her fingers. Then he shrugged.

'All right. If you insist.'

While he was downstairs Hester set to in the gleaming kitchen, her professional eye gloating over the various appliances while she despatched the washing up. It was a dream kitchen, with everything planned for efficiency down to the last detail. Cooking in these surroundings would be a joy. Except that any woman who was mistress of a kitchen like this would never need to cook for a living, she reminded herself sharply. Almost furtively Hester opened the drawers and cupboards to find the correct homes for crockery and cutlery, taking in the ceramic hob and built-in oven with a wistful eye. She looked up, startled, to see John in the doorway, watching her.

'Can I tear you away from the frenzy of tidying up?' he asked, a glint of amusement in his eyes.

Hester put down the dishcloth she was holding and dried her hands.

'I was just admiring all the gadgetry,' she said. 'A professional interest, as it were.'

'I'm glad you approve. Let's have a drink.'

As they crossed the hall together Hester was prey to a vague uneasiness. The entire day seemed to have been spent in an unavoidable atmosphere of domesticity it seemed impossible to ignore.

'Was Jo asleep?' she asked, and sat down near the newly made-up fire.

'Like an angel. I let Scrap out for a moment and she's back in her basket now, settled down with Jo for the night.' John kicked a log more securely into the flames. 'What can I offer you, Hester?'

'I don't know that I really want anything,' she said, thinking of the bourbon earlier, 'unless it's something a lot more innocuous than the drink you made me this morning.'

John laughed and crossed the room to the drinks cabinet. 'I'll concoct something very pleasant for you, I promise.'

Hester felt a vague sense of unreality as she sat quietly, looking round her at the big, attractive room. The only light came from the crackling fire and the two lamps on the sofa tables, the great expanse of raw silk curtain across the windows enclosing them in a cocoon which was none the less intimate for its sweeping dimensions. She took the glass he handed her and eyed it warily.

'What is it this time, Jack?'

'Just a blend of fruit juices with a dash of brandy.'

He lowered himself beside her on the soft suede of the couch, not close enough for contact, but too near for Hester to relax properly. She sipped at her drink, finding it very pleasant, and leaned back against the cushions, giving a surreptitious glance at her watch.

'It's just after nine, Hester,' John informed her drily. 'Rather early for bedtime, even by your stringent standards.'

'I'm sorry,' she said defensively. 'I don't mean to be rude. No doubt the women you're used to would be perfectly at ease under these circumstances, but frankly I find it impossible. This particular situation is a trifle bizarre, don't you agree?'

He finished the brandy in his glass and put it down before turning towards her, his eyes very bright under the half-lowered lids that gave him the indefinable air of surperiority Hester found so irritating.

'Bizarre? What's wrong with a husband and wife sitting at home in front of the fire while their child sleeps peacefully in bed?' he asked mockingly.

'Nothing, until you add the prefixes. It's ex-husband and ex-wife, and it's your home, not mine.'

'The descriptions don't apply even then, Hester.' John's face hardened, his eyes suddenly ice-cold. 'The term ex-husband implies that once I was actually a husband. And that's a pleasure I've never been granted, unless you count those visits in the hospital—and please don't bring up the unhappy accident of our first encounter. Although I still regret it, in one way, I consider I've grovelled and apologised more than enough since then, and anyway, I don't pretend to regret the circumstances that brought Jo into the world.'

'Naturally not, since you weren't the one left holding the baby!' Hester's eyes flashed green, like an angry tigress.

'I was always willing to shoulder my responsibilities, Hester,' he reminded her smoothly, 'but obviously the idea of me as a husband was more unacceptable to you than life as a single parent. Was I so physically repellant to you?'

'No.' Hester met his eyes levelly. 'But that doesn't mean anything, Jack. And if it's an oblique reference to the incident this afternoon, well, I'm just not accustomed to physical attentions from a man, and—and they were rather pleasant, I'll grant you. But that's all it was. Put it down to human frailty, if you like.'

John's eyes emptied of expression until they were blank as glass, and he got to his feet, sauntering across the room for more brandy.

'You surprise me, Hester,' he threw over his shoulder, 'I was unaware you had any frailties. May I top up your drink?'

'No thank you.' The atmosphere between them suddenly crackled with tension, and Hester sought desperately for some way to relieve it. 'Do you still play chess?' she asked in desperation.

John returned to sit opposite her. 'No. I rarely have the time. And if I do there's never an opponent available. Why? Would you like a game?'

What Hester really wanted was escape; to get away from him and shut herself up in one of the guest rooms for the night, but chess seemed a better idea than sniping at each other for the rest of the evening.

'I haven't played since—since I was in the hospital,' she said quietly. 'I don't remember much about the rules, I'm afraid.'

'How odd, since you like rules so much.' John's voice was acid as he got up. 'I'm sure you'll pick it up again quite easily. It might even soothe your ruffled nerves.'

'My nerves are perfectly normal, thank you.'

'Rubbish! You look like a sacrificial lamb sitting there, as though you expect me to pounce on you at any moment. You can set your mind at rest, I assure you. My intentions are strictly honourable.' John smiled at her with irritating superiority. 'Perhaps a lesson—in chess—would be therapeutic.'

'Or I could just go to bed,' said Hester with asperity, and drained her glass. 'I'm sure you can provide me with a book.'

John ignored her, taking a large box from a carved wooded chest near the fireplace. He pulled up a small table between the couches and handed the box to Hester. 'Go on,' he prompted. 'Open it.'

Hester smoothed her fingers over the inlaid wood of the lid before raising it to discover the most exquisitely carved chess pieces she had ever seen. She lifted out a queen with reverence, turning it over in her fingers in delight. 'Ivory?' she asked.

'Yes. The lady's very beautiful, don't you agree, despite her age—which is considerable.' John took the box from her and set the pieces up on the table, then settled himself opposite. 'Now then, Hester, let's see how much you remember.'

At first it was humiliatingly little, but as the time wore on some of the basic moves began to return and at the end of an hour Hester at least had some idea of what she ought to be doing. In her absorption she hardly noticed when John got up to replenish the fire and refill her glass, only a muttered word of thanks issuing from behind her furious concentration. When John once again said 'checkmate' Hester stretched wearily, then caught sight of the time with a gasp.

'It's gone midnight,' she said guiltily. 'Jo—I should have gone down to see her——'

'She's fine,' said John reassuringly. 'I looked in on her when I fetched more logs. You hardly seemed to notice I was gone.'

'I do apologise.' Hester stood up and looked at him awkwardly. 'If you'll tell me which room I'm to use I'll go to bed.'

'Not for a moment, Hester. Sit down again and have another drink.' He pushed her gently back on the sofa while he put away the chess set. Hester watched him through narrowed eyes.

'I don't want another drink, Jack.'

'As you wish.' He sat beside her and took her hand, turning her towards him. 'Hester, I have something to say, and I'd like you to try to hear me out to the end. Then you can say all you want; but at first please listen. Will you?'

Eyes dark with suspicion Hester nodded reluctantly, and he leaned back, her hand still loosely clasped in his.

'Frankly, Hester,' he began, 'I'm deeply disturbed about Jo.'

She stiffened, and tried to withdraw her hand, but he tightened his grasp, and she subsided, keeping silent with an effort.

'Admittedly she was kidnapped by mistake,' he went on, his face sombre as he stared into the fire, 'but in view of my—my financial standing we can't rule out the possibility of it happening for real some other time, unless we take suitable precautions.'

Hester drew in a deep breath, chilled by his words.

'And what do you consider "suitable precautions"?' she asked carefully.

'Let's leave that for the moment. What concerns me most immediately is her state of mind. The thought of returning to your house is obviously frightening her to death.' He turned to look at her. 'When she first came home she was just relieved to be back, and I was there to lunch, and then you had a shopping spree, and finally she was pretty well worn out with excitement as well as the fright she'd had, so she slept well enough last night. But since then she's had time to think. Jo's a very bright child, and now it's occurred to her that what happened once could happen again, as you could see by what she said earlier. The fact that she was taken by mistake has no significance in her eyes. It all happened to *her*, and she's terrified it will happen again.'

'But surely that will pass! Children are very

adaptable, Jack. She's bound to get over it sooner or later.' This sounded lame even to Hester, but she was very apprehensive of any solution John was about to make.

'And if it's later?' His eyes were steel hard. 'Are you prepared to see her hysterical with fright every night at bedtime, then again every morning when it's time for school? Because I'm very much afraid that's how she's going to react. Good God, Hester, I had nightmares as a child after seeing some stupid film about monsters. How do you expect a little scrap like Jo to behave when the ultimate horror of abduction has actually happened to her?'

'Stop it, stop it!' Hester tore her hand from his and hunched over, tears welling from her eyes. 'Do you think I've given no thought at all to this? I lay awake most of last night afraid that Jo would have a nightmare, or cry for me in the night. I was wracked with guilt because I wasn't there at school when I should have been—a fact you've reminded me of several times!' She halted, the tears getting the upper hand, and silently John put a handkerchief in her hand. Hester scrubbed at her eyes and blew her nose, careless of how she looked. Breathing deeply in an attempt at calm she turned to face him, her eyes suspicious beneath swollen lids. 'So what do you have in mind, Jack? No doubt you have some plan of action ready and waiting. What do you propose?'

'Propose is exactly the word,' he answered, his face carefully blank. 'I think we should get married again, Hester.'

She stared at him. 'What good will that do?'

'It will solve everything.' His voice was deliberately matter-of-fact as he resisted her efforts to elude the hand he laid on hers. 'Listen, Hester, please.'

'I'm listening,' she said militantly, and turned away to look into the fire.

'You said earlier you had no wish to marry anyone else.' John put a hand under her chin, forcing her to look at him. 'Did you mean it?'

She nodded. 'Yes. I meant it.'

'If you marry me you can regard it as a business arrangement,' he said briskly. 'I provide you and Jo with a home, which, in essence, is all I ask in return. I want a home to return to at night, instead of just a house. And I want to watch my daughter growing up, instead of the small doses of Jo's company I'm allowed at present. And perhaps you and I could learn to live together in some sort of amicable relationship. No demands on my part, physical or otherwise. I'm away quite a lot, which brings me to the next thing. Alicia would be welcome to make her home here too, of course. I've no wish to disrupt your present way of life, Hester.'

Hester gazed at him, fighting the impulse to laugh hysterically. No wish to disrupt her life, indeed! John Lauder Ransome had done nothing else from the first disastrous moment of their meeting.

'And how would this arrangement provide more security for Jo?' she asked coolly.

'For one thing she'd have a different address with an unlisted telephone number, and for another I'd take her away from that school,' he said grimly. 'And if we were together, as a family, I think most of her anxiety would just naturally disappear.'

Hester turned away, and sat in silence, mulling over his proposition in her mind. 'You've thought it all out very thoroughly,' she said presently. 'I've been thinking of the same problem, too. It was running round and round in my mind all night.'

'But of course my solution to it would never have occurred to you in a million years,' he said caustically, and laid her hand back on her knee.

'No,' Hester agreed, 'but now it's been put before me may I have time to think about it?'

'Of course.' John got to his feet and began raking the fire together, his back to her, something in the set of his shoulders indicating his displeasure very plainly.

'Perhaps you could let me have your decision in the morning.'

Hester grimaced, unseen. It sounded as if they were discussing some business merger, instead of the highly emotive rearrangement of their entire existence.

'Yes, I will,' she said colourlessly, and got up, collecting her wrap from the other couch, and looking round for her handbag and boots. 'I really would like to get some rest now, if you'd just show me where I'm to sleep.'

John put the fireguard in place then took her boots from her hand and waved her ahead of him through the door. Hester felt like a prisoner under escort to the dungeons as she preceded him down the spiral stair, and wished he would say something to break the silence. He paused at the open door of Jo's room, and they both watched their sleeping child for some time. She lay on her stomach, one arm hanging over the edge of the bed, her hand within reach of the basket where Scrap lay snoring softly. John took Hester's arm and drew her gently towards the next door, opening it and turning on the light in the adjoining room, which was very attractive, decorated in shades of citrus and white like the bathroom she had used earlier.

'If you leave the door ajar you can hear her if she calls,' said John quietly, and eyed her doubtfully. 'I don't think I possess anything suitable in the way of nightwear to offer you.'

'I could roll up the arms and legs of a pair of your pyjamas,' she suggested with a little smile.

His lips twitched. 'Sorry. Not something I own, I'm afraid.'

Hester coloured to the roots of her hair, and turned away.

'I'll manage,' she said in a stifled voice. 'Good night.'

'Good night, Hester. Try to get some sleep.' John stood irresolute for a moment, his eyes brooding on her averted face, then he went quietly from the room.

Hester did her best to follow his advice, but John's proposition made it very difficult to sleep. With one ear alert to listen for Jo, and her brain in a turmoil at the thought of living here permanently as John's wife, Hester twisted and turned in the comfortable bed, wide-eyed as she stared into the darkness. Half of her was all for the idea, the half that was tired of a life of endless cooking with only Jo and her mother for company. The other half of Hester was very wary indeed about giving herself up into John Ransome's keeping. Once should have been enough. To marry him a second time was a bit much, a shade too final for comfort. Admittedly the first time had been on paper only—mere marriage lines entitling herself and her baby to the name of Ransome, also the fragile veil of respectability obviously doubted in the neighbourhood where she lived. The regular visits to the house by John's impressive car, once Jo was old enough, had been Hester's saving grace, had she cared for public opinion, and to her mortification she had. At first the attitude of several elderly ladies in the vicinity had been wounding. It was plain that they considered the tale of a husband apocryphal and her married name assumed. Hester did her best to ignore them, telling herself their opinions were unimportant, that heaps of women chose to bring up children alone in this enlightened age. The fact remained, however. In her neck of the woods this outlook was frowned on, and husbands considered mandatory appendages to mother-hood.

But how would it feel to live in this big, beautiful house, with a man coming home in the evenings, and no deep-seated need to earn the money that bought her independence? Hester had no answer. For Jo the advantages were enormous, that much was clear. Her child very plainly loved it here, and loved her father too, however Hester had tried to delude herself otherwise. She turned over on her stomach and sighed. She herself liked it here, for that matter. It was a house she could live in only too easily. But Hester was secretly needled by the way John had framed his proposal. She would have found his offer a lot more palatable if he had desired her not only under his roof but in his bed, so that she could have refused the latter with dignity and laid down the terms of acceptance herself. As things were the proposed change was more like moving house than getting married. Only the address would be different, even the name would be the same.

Hester tensed as a slight, muffled sound reach her in the darkness. She sprang out of bed, fumbling for the light-switch, and ran to Jo's room. A little heaving mound lay in the middle of the bed, threshing around in blankets which smothered the sound of tearing sobs, Scrap whining in distress, her paws on the edge of the bed. Hester tore the covers away from Jo and caught hold of her with difficulty, the child fighting her off like a wildcat until she realised where she was and collapsed sobbing against Hester's shoulder.

'It's all right, Baby,' soothed Hester, rocking the little body in her arms as John burst through the door, his face white.

'Is she——?'

'Bad dream,' answered Hester briefly, and sat down with Jo in her lap. John sat beside her, stroking the damp, short hair, his face grim with anxiety as Jo gradually calmed down.

'What was it, sweetheart?' he asked gently.

'Man came—blanket——' hiccuped Jo, her eyes still tightly shut.

'No he didn't, darling,' said Hester calmly. 'There's only Daddy and me here. You got tangled up in the bedcovers, that's all, and now you've woken up poor Scrap. Look how worried she is.'

Jo's eyes opened like magic, such an overwhelming look of relief flooding her face at the sight of her parents and the dog Hester's throat constricted. John clicked his fingers and the little dog jumped up to lick

Jo's face. Her tears dried like magic as she spluttered, giggling, trying to avoid the dog's tongue.

'It tickles, Scrap! Stop it,' she gurgled, and Hester felt limp with relief at Jo's abrupt transition from tears to laughter.

'Perhaps Daddy could wash your face properly,' she said prosaically, and set Jo on her feet. 'I'll tidy your bed.'

John swung the little pyjama-clad figure up in his arms and carried her into the bathroom, exchanging a level look with Hester over Jo's head. Hester straightened the rumpled bed and tucked in the covers firmly, filled with a sense of inevitability, already resigned to the fact that her mind had been made up for her. If Jo felt like this in the safety of John's house, heaven knew how she was likely to react back in Orchard Crescent. Hester could hear John and Jo laughing together in the bathroom, and had a smile ready on her own face as they came back and the tired little girl was tucked up once more.

As John stooped to kiss his drowsy little daughter, Hester's eyes were drawn to the muscular length of his legs beneath the rather ancient towelling robe he wore. She gave a quick glance down at the shortcomings of her own garb, suddenly embarrassed at the brevity of her satin slip as John stood up. Jo's eyes opened fully for a moment and looked up in enquiry at her father.

'Are you sleeping in Mummy's bed tonight, Daddy? Like Belinda's Mummy and Daddy?'

For once John was nonplussed. It was a moment or two before he collected himself sufficiently to answer.

'Not tonight, darling. I might—disturb her.' There was a very odd note in his voice, and he avoided Hester's eyes as she bent to kiss Jo.

'Go to sleep now, Baby,' she said, glad to hide her scarlet cheeks. 'I'm just next door, remember.'

'Not a baby,' mumbled Jo indistinctly, already half asleep as her parents tip-toed from the room together.

John followed Hester into the other room and closed the door behind him. He leaned against it, looking at her, hands in the pockets of his robe. Now the excitement was over Hester felt ill-at-ease, very conscious of dishevelled hair and scanty petticoat. She sat on the edge of the bed and wished John would leave. The sight of him with tousled hair and tanned legs bare to the thigh was making her nervous.

'Are you all right, Hester?' he asked at last.

She knew he was looking at her, but just nodded, her eyes on her bare toes.

'Yes. I'm fine.'

'Would you like a drink, or tea perhaps?'

'No, thank you.'

John's mouth tightened as Hester's eyes remained lowered.

'I'll say good night, then. I hope Jo stays asleep until morning.'

'I'm sure she will. Normally she never stirs.' Hester glanced up to meet the caustic gleam in John's eyes.

'One can hardly class the present situation as normal,' he said.

'No. But she'll get over it in time,' she said with conviction.

'And in the interim?'

'I'll move in here as you suggested.'

John stared at her, frowning.

'That wasn't precisely what I meant, Hester.'

'I know what you meant,' she said collectedly. 'I hadn't been to sleep when Jo woke. I spent the time thinking over what you said about the after-effects on her, and so on, and came to the conclusion that you were right. The incident just now merely underlined it.' She looked at him unwaveringly. 'The last thing I want is to marry you, Jack. I might as well be honest. But under the circumstances it seems I must, if only to provide Jo with a background she can believe in as safe. In time I'm sure you and I will manage to work out a reasonably friendly relationship—I won't even expect you to curtail any other relationships you have, as long as you use discretion—'

'How very magnanimous of you,' he cut in, the drawl in his voice very pronounced. 'So I may take it you're ready to bestow your hand, if not your heart, in marriage, Hester. When?'

There was a look in John's ice-cold eyes Hester disliked intensely.

'Perhaps we can leave the details for a more civilised hour,' she said. 'I'm a little weary.'

'Of course.' John went to the door at once, then paused. 'Try to sleep as long as possible. I shan't go in to the works tomorrow—I can see to Jo if she wakes early.'

'Will the firm function without you?' she asked mockingly.

John shrugged, his eyes expressionless once more.

'No one's indispensible. Good night.'

'Good night.'

Hester sat looking down at her bare toes for some time after the door closed softly behind John, then she went to look at Jo for a moment before returning to bed. As she stretched out beneath the covers she could feel her body relaxing almost at once. Now the decision had been made her brain obviously considered its work was over for the time being and she could sleep.

CHAPTER SEVEN

HESTER married John again with their beaming daughter as bridesmaid. The only guests were Alicia and Lucy, Camilla and Mike Desmond and John's parents, who had flown over from Portugal for the occasion. The numbers were a considerable increase on the first time round, but even so Hester found the occasion just as nerve-racking as that other far off time when she had been so ill she had barely known what was happening. She arrived at the Registry Office with all the *joie de vivre* normally reserved for a visit to the dentist. When the details had been discussed beforehand the ceremony itself had somehow seemed like just another item on a list to be dealt with in the new 'arrangement', which was how she privately regarded her new life. During the car ride on the day itself Hester began to have misgivings. The ceremony loomed in front of her like the north face of the Eiger, and she was sorry she had ever agreed to the whole thing. It would have been so much simpler just to move into John's house and leave it at that. The end result would have been the same. She had, in fact, broached the idea to him, but his response had been an ultimatum, and cold. Marriage or nothing. She had given in, and John had promptly taken himself off on a protracted trip to the Far East, leaving Hester and Jo at Prospect, with Alicia to keep them company, and visits from a delighted Camilla almost every day.

Alicia had no intention of making her home permanently at Prospect, to Hester's regret. After the wedding she was returning to her own house, and the life that went with it. She preferred surroundings that were comfortable and familiar, with her friend Barbara

125

Drayton for company at the bridge club and upholstery classes, and the regular visits to the cinema and the theatre. Alicia had been very understanding about Jo's fear of living at Orchard Crescent after her abduction, indeed had even anticipated the child's reaction. Jo had tried very hard to explain to her grandmother how she felt, doing her best to persuade Alicia to live with them at Prospect, as John had originally suggested, but Alicia was gently adamant.

'I shall be perfectly happy here, Jo, and you can come and visit me with Mummy, and I shall visit you. Just like Belinda and her Grandma.'

Jo's troubled face had cleared instantly, and she had plunged wholeheartedly into the task of helping Hester pack all her own treasures and belongings to take to 'Daddy's house'. Hester's eyes softened as they rested on Jo's animated face as she chattered to her grandmother and Lucy in the car. The cropped hair had grown a little, and lay in feathery curls close to the small head above the velvet collar of the new winter coat which hid the splendour of Jo's bridesmaid's dress, an apple green corded velvet affair with a knot of dark green ribbons at the waist. Hester had been apathetic about her own choice of clothes, only Alicia's urging prompting her to buy the grey flannel coat with velvet collar, that looked so like a school uniform Alicia herself paid for the vivid scrap of emerald velvet and ribbons for Hester to wear on her head. The result was elegance rather than severity, and Hester was glad of it when she arrived at the Registrar's office and made the acquaintance of John's parents, who were not unnaturally curious about the young woman their son was marrying for the second time. They were reassuringly kind and welcoming, which Hester felt was very forbearing under the circumstances, and immediately enamoured of Jo, who chattered away artlessly to everyone in such tremendous spirits that this alone made the whole affair worth the trouble from her mother's point of view.

The short exchange of vows was quickly over, as was the unexpected photographic session arranged by John. Looking tall and remote in one of his elegant grey suits, he held Hester's arm in a relentless grip in the small, pleasant garden at the back of the building, while a photographer immortalised the event on film, after which the assembled company enjoyed a convivial lunch together in the private dining-room of the Bear, once a coaching inn, and now in the good food guide. After the meal everyone divided up into different combinations for the journey home. John's idea had been for a short holiday somewhere for a honeymoon, but this had been instantly vetoed by Hester. Her reasons had been numerous, but the one she gave was her reluctance to leave Jo, and as neither of them fancied the idea of a honeymoon with a five-year-old child in tow, however beloved, the subject was dropped. Hester felt flat and depressed at the prospect of the evening ahead, which would be spent in the same way as all the other evenings of their future, presumably. She stole a quick look at John's profile as he drove them back through the fading light of the November afternoon. He looked detached and withdrawn, and feeling vaguely chilled, Hester looked over at the back seat where Jo was dozing, still clutching the nosegay of flowers John had given her when he presented Hester with a spray of pink rosebuds to pin to her collar. She settled deeper into her seat, turning her head to sniff the roses, and gave a little shiver.

'Are you cold?' John glanced at her and pushed the heating switch to 'high'.

'A little.'

'Your coat hardly seems warm enough for this kind of weather.'

'One tends to lean more towards appearance than comfort on occasions like this.'

'Or indeed on any other occasion, Hester, as far as you're concerned,' he put in smoothly.

Hester shot him a resentful green look.

'At least,' she said sweetly, 'my outfit is a great improvement on the maternity dress of first time round.'

After that the rest of the journey passed in silence, and it was a pale, headachey bride who emerged from the Daimler when it drew up in the drive at Prospect. John woke Jo gently, and let her out of the car to run calling to Scrap and Mrs Denham, giving the house-keeper an excited account of the day's events. The latter had a tea-trolley ready to wheel in front of the blazing fire in the living-room, a smile of pride on her kind face as she produced a small iced wedding-cake to place alongside the plate of muffins waiting to be toasted.

'Why Mrs Denham,' said Hester, touched. 'How very sweet of you.'

'Not very professional, by your standards, Mrs Ransome, but there's only good things in it, so it shouldn't taste too bad.' The woman's face glowed with pleasure as Jo cooed over the ribboned cake with delight.

'Look, Mummy, it's got blue writing!'

'It says "Good Luck",' said John, leaning over to see. 'That's why Denny's put a little silver horseshoe on top, Jo, as a good luck symbol.'

They were likely to need plenty of that, thought Hester, and unpinned the hat, glad to be rid of the ostrich plume that had irritated her all afternoon. She let Mrs Denham take her coat and sat close to the fire, shivering in the grey silk dress she had worn for the ceremony, feeling suddenly shy and awkward, and deeply thankful for Jo's presence as Mrs Denham left them to enjoy their tea and went home. John had returned from Hong Kong only two days previously, and had spent the intervening time with Camilla and his parents. Now the three of them were together as a family for the first time, as he had said he wanted, and

Hester felt ill-at-ease, trying to accustom herself to the idea that from now on this would be her home and her life. She faced the prospect with a feeling perilously near to panic. She and Alicia had been sleeping here for the past weeks, admittedly, but during the day Jo had started at the new school just outside the village, an experience she was enjoying immensely, and Hester had been busy with the transfer of belongings from Orchard Crescent to Prospect, also with helping Alain Girardin out with desserts until he had found someone to take over the job. This last Hester had kept from John, with the idea of keeping the peace, but she had welcomed the work as something to keep her occupied, to stop her thinking and worrying too much about the new arrangement. I must stop alluding to my marriage as an arrangement, Hester thought, frowning, and started as John said her name loudly. He was standing near the fire, toasting fork in hand, looking at her rather oddly.

'I asked if you'd pour out, Hester, while Jo and I get on with the toasting,' he said, with the air of one who's said it all before.

Hester smiled at him brightly.

'Yes, of course. Be careful of your dress, Jo.'

' 'Course I will—can I hold the fork, Daddy?' Jo's blazingly happy face turned up to John, and he nodded.

'Only gently does it, sweetheart, don't get too near the heat, and mind Scrap doesn't get at the muffins.' Heedless of his expensive grey trousers he went down on his knees beside her and kept close watch on the operation.

Hester accepted the first muffin with ceremony, not because she was hungry, but to please Jo, and ate a little of it and drank a great deal of tea while the other two polished off an amazing quantity, considering the elegant lunch consumed only a short time before. Cutting the wedding cake was the next hurdle, and after watching Hester try to eat her slice John said casually,

'Why not go downstairs and have a rest? Jo and I will

clear up, and then I'll watch television with her for a while.'

Their eyes met over Jo's head, but John's were unreadable as usual, and Hester turned away, nodding.

'Thank you. I think I will. O.K. by you, Jo?'

Jo nodded, smiling, only too delighted to have her father to herself obviously, and feeling a trifle extraneous Hester picked up her hat and bag and went across to the door John held open for her.

'Try to sleep,' he advised.

'Yes, I intend to. I feel a bit tired.'

'Not sleeping well lately?'

'No. But I'll get back to normal in a while, I'm sure.'

John gave a quick glance at Jo. She was busily tidying the tea-trolley, and he turned back to Hester.

'Do you realise I have no idea what "normal" is for you, Hester? During most of the time we've spent in each other's company you've either been ill, or half-crazed with worry.'

Hester smiled involuntarily, making a little face.

'That sounds terrible. I'm very average, Jack, I'm afraid; boringly so. You'll probably find me exceedingly dull.'

He shook his head. 'I doubt that very much. Now get some rest, you look tired.'

Hester went downstairs feeling comforted. Perhaps they would be able to make a good life together as friends rather than lovers, which conclusion made her feel unexpectedly wistful, and she took a book to bed with her to read instead of trying to sleep.

Jo went happily to bed later that evening, accompanied by the faithful Scrap, and afterwards Hester and John sat together and watched a documentary on television. She had changed into comfortable corduroy slacks and heavy wool sweater, and felt much more relaxed. After the programme finished John switched off the set and put some piano music on the stereo while Hester read the paper. Eventually she asked him for a pen, and he put down the *Financial Times* and went over to a writing desk near the window, returning with a ball-point pen.

'What are you doing?' he asked, and sat beside her.

'Crossword. I love them.' She gave him a bright, considering look. 'Perhaps it might be an idea to have a quiz—find out each other's likes and dislikes.'

John's face took on an irritatingly superior expression as he leaned back, his legs stretched out comfortably in front of him.

'I already know something of yours. I used to pump your mother so I could make the right offerings in hospital.'

Hester laughed involuntarily.

'Cheat! I used to wonder how I got opera tapes and historical novels with such unerring accuracy. And all the time I thought it was your perspicacity.'

'No. Just ingenuity.' He leaned over. 'Fifteen across is "dryad", by the way.'

'So it is. Thanks.'

'To revert to your likes and dislikes,' John went on. 'You love steak and hate liver, prefer fruit to chocolates, television plays to situation comedies, like most forms of music, but opera best, and prefer casual to formal clothes.'

Hester stared at him in admiration.

'How on earth did you remember all that?'

His smile was smug.

'I possess that sort of mind. What do you know about me?'

Hester thought hard for a moment, then looked at him guiltily.

'Hardly anything, Jack. I was too full of resentment originally, then when—I mean after the divorce I did my best never to think of you at all.'

He nodded in resignation.

'That's what I thought. And since? Be honest—my back is broad.'

'You're clever, successful, popular with women, have a superb tailor and barber—or does one say hairdresser nowadays?'

'Barber will do.'

'I know you're good at relationships, too. Thoughtful son, good brother, and absolutely number one in the father ratings in Jo's eyes.' Hester stopped as John's fingers closed over one of her hands.

'Never mind all that, Hester,' he said abruptly. 'What kind of rating do I merit in *your* beautiful green eyes?'

Hester felt a little flustered, and kept the eyes in question on her linked hands.

'Well, I—I don't feel any animosity about the original *contretemps* any more,' she said with care, and wondered how to go on. She could hardly say she was no longer consumed with jealousy for Laura Verney now that lady was safely married. The less said on that particular subject the better.

'Is that all, Hester?' John's voice sounded flat, and she hastened to remedy the deficit.

'What I'm trying to say, Jack, is that I don't see why our marriage shouldn't be a success if we genuinely work at it.'

She could feel his withdrawal even before he took his hand away and stood up.

'Yes, of course. I agree. Now shall we make a start on the meal Mrs Denham left for us?'

Hester was conscious she had failed to say what John had expected, and sat down to the meal feeling somewhat at a loss. If only he would allow his feelings to show a little more she might have more idea of what he wanted her to say. It was too late at this particular juncture, that was obvious, and over the meal she followed his lead and kept to impersonal topics. John was interested to know how the hotel had taken her resignation from the role of dessert chef.

'Very well. Alain was very pleased for me.' Hester paused for a moment, eyeing him uncertainly. 'Actually

I did carry on cooking for a week or so until he found someone else.' To her relief John grinned.

'All right, Hester, don't look so guilty. I shan't bite you.'

Hester frowned.

'I do seem to annoy you rather easily though, Jack. You can't blame me for treading warily.'

His eyes danced with genuine amusement.

'Likewise, Hester. I manage to strike sparks off you quite easily, too. Perhaps we should start our new life together with a new resolution to be pleasant to each other on all possible occasions.'

Hester laughed outright.

'We can make the resolution easily enough. Keeping it will be the problem!'

John lifted his wine glass.

'Let's drink to it, then, Hester.' He smiled deliberately into her eyes over the silver candelabra between them on the table. 'To peace.'

'To peace,' she echoed, and drank from her glass. 'By the way, Jack, how did Miss Beauchamp react when you told her you were taking Jo away from the school?'

He snorted.

'She had the nerve to be affronted! Called Jo's kidnap "an unfortunate misunderstanding", would you believe. She even hinted that if you'd been there it would never have happened.'

Hester paused, fork half-way to her mouth.

'Which is true.'

'I don't agree,' he answered emphatically, 'apart from which I let her know in no uncertain terms that no one criticises my wife in my hearing.' His face looked menacing as he pushed his plate aside.

'What did she say to that?'

'Oh, she apologised, of course, very much conscious of the "adverse publicity to the school", to use her own words, if the affair was made common knowledge.'

Hester took their plates to the sideboard and

returned to the table with the cheeseboard.

'That's what she said to me when I rang her the Friday Jo went missing.'

'Cold-blooded harpy! She was quite happy when she realised I wasn't demanding a return of the fees, and we parted forthwith.' He offered her the celery. 'And Jo loves the new school, she tells me.'

'She does. She missed her friend Belinda at first, but Jo's such an outgoing child she soon made other friends. I was really very impressed by the educational standard. That young headmaster has some very go-ahead ideas.'

John made coffee while Hester cleared away, still talking about the school, and eventually they returned to the living-room to watch a play on television. They sat together on one of the couches, drinking the coffee-pot dry, as relaxed and comfortable as though this were one of a hundred other evenings spent in the same way, and it was only when the inevitable explicit love scene occurred on the screen towards the end of the play that Hester experienced any qualms. John gave no sign of similar reaction, but stayed quiet and attentive right to the end.

'Best play I've seen for some time,' he remarked, and switched off the set. 'Now, Hester, what kind of music would you like? And don't ask for anything too highbrow!'

She laughed, and picked up the crossword.

'Philistine! I really don't mind, Jack. More piano music, if you like.'

As the sophisticated sound of George Shearing's piano came stealing through the room she nodded in approval and went on juggling with an anagram, looking up with a smile as a cork popped a moment later and John handed her a brimming glass.

'Champagne, Jack?' Hester sipped with appreciation.

John sat down beside her, leaning across to toss the newspaper aside.

'Let's forget about crosswords for tonight,' he said, and raised his glass to her. 'A toast, Hester. To us; you, me and Jo.'

'To us,' she echoed, and drank obediently, meeting his eyes over the rim of the glass.

John took it from her and laid it down with his, then pulled her into his arms so casually his mouth was against hers before she had time to think about it. Instead of thinking she responded, her body curving into his with an unselfconscious ardour that made his breath catch, his own body quickening instantly. One of his hands twisted into her hair, holding her still while his lips and tongue gave such definitive pleasure Hester felt a reaction run through her veins like quicksilver, heat arrowing to her nipples and the pit of her stomach, and lower. John made no move to caress her further. He just held her close against his body, which she could feel was as fully aroused as hers, but still he retained his rigid self-control until Hester could have begged him to stop, or go on, or do anything to relieve the tension at breaking point inside her. At last he raised his head and looked down at her with eyes lit by such a molten gleam she marvelled she had ever thought them cold. Dark colour emphasized his cheekbónes, and the thick blond hair was falling over his sweat-dampened forehead as he lay against her in silent intimacy, still holding her close while their ragged breathing slowed, and their bodies gradually relaxed.

'Is that sort of thing against the rules for making our marriage a success?' he asked lazily, and smoothed the curls from her forehead with a possessive hand.

Hester's eyes fell before the look in his.

'I assumed a more platonic arrangement was what we had in mind,' she muttered.

'What *you* had in mind, Hester.' John put a finger under her chin and forced her to meet his eyes. 'A mere male, like me, tends to regrettable lapses towards the more carnal, I'm afraid. Surely you admit that one can be good friends *and* enjoy a normal physical relationship. It's not necessary to be madly in love, you know.'

Hester moved away and sat up straight.

'Of course. I'm not straight out of the egg.' She felt disorientated after soaring to such heights, only to be pulled down to earth with a bump. She reached for her glass. 'Perhaps I could have some more champagne.'

'Of course.' John retrieved their glasses and filled them. 'What shall we drink to this time?'

Hester took the glass from him, looking thoughtful.

'To friendship, Jack?'

'In other words, sweet bride, I'm to keep off the grass.' He gave her a derisive smile, and drank the contents of his glass all at once.

Hester curled up comfortably on the couch and smiled back, her composure hard won, but quite passable, under the circumstances.

'I think we'll do better at establishing a reasonable relationship if we don't fog it up with other issues, Jack. You must admit that for two people entering into marriage for the second time we hardly know each other at all. Let's take things sensibly, a step at a time; really learn to know each other.'

'Without any recourse to the biblical sense of the word, of course!' he said bitingly.

'If you must reduce it to basics, yes.'

'Most people do, Hester, believe me.' John went over to the cabinet and took out a bottle of single malt whisky. 'Can I offer you anything else?'

'No thanks.' She looked with disapproval at the whisky bottle, and he turned, noting her expression.

'One glass of whisky won't turn me into a raging beast, I assure you,' he said caustically.

'Past experience makes me wary,' she said nastily. 'I can be forgiven for feeling nervous, surely.'

There was silence while John regarded her with an expression that made her shift in her seat uneasily.

'Oh yes, Hester, *you* can be forgiven,' he said wearily. 'A shame it doesn't work both ways.' He returned the whisky bottle to the cabinet unopened, then went over to the fire and raked it together, put the guard in place and gave Hester a formal little nod. 'I think I'll call it a day, then. Good night.'

'Good night,' said Hester, dismayed, the wind taken from her sails completely. Her eyes were wide and forlorn as they followed the tall, graceful figure across the room. John went through the door without a backward glance, and she sat quite still in the quiet room, which now she was alone in it seemed twice its former size. She picked up the crossword and doggedly filled in a few more clues, then gave it up and took the champagne flutes to the kitchen instead, carefully washing and drying the intricately cut crystal before replacing them in the cabinet in the living room. She drew back the curtains and switched off the lights, standing at the great window for some time, just gazing out at the stars. Then she went slowly down the spiral stair to Jo's room, replacing the covers that had fallen off and smoothing the hair away from the small, sleeping face. She gave Scrap a pat and went through to her own room, where a lamp was on beside the bed, and a large package lay, conspicuous, on the duvet. Hester unwrapped it and stood in silence, biting her lip. Inside was a large, beautifully illustrated cookery book, and with it the video of Zefirelli's film version of the opera *Traviata*. Her wedding present from Jack, presumably. Hester felt small. It suddenly seemed ungenerous, silly even, to keep her husband at arms length.

Hester hugged her arms round herself, and paced round the room, her heart heavy. Her stupid pride had prompted her to opt for a platonic relationship. The rest of her had clamoured to be Jack's wife in every sense of the word, until he made the mistake of telling her love was unnecessary when it came to enjoying the delights of the connubial couch. Then she had wanted to hit back. She suddenly seemed to want a lot of things, not least of which was for Jack to want *her*, and for herself alone, not because she came as one of a pair with Jo. Which was crying for the moon, presumably, so it would seem sensible to settle for what she had. Hester brushed furiously at her wildly tangled hair and paid meticulous attention to her face and, after a moment's hesitation, put on the new silk nightgown. She slid into bed, and lay leafing blindly through the pages of the glossy new book, but tonight food failed to hold her interest. She put the heavy book down on her bedside table and lay with hands behind her head, staring at the wall. John had said he would demand nothing, and he had kept to it. He had kissed her on two occasions only up to the present, which could hardly be termed excessive, particularly when she had responded to him in no uncertain manner each time. In which case why was she behaving like such a wet, she asked herself irritably, and threw back the duvet, almost running to the door before she could change her mind. Outside in the hallway it was dark, with no glimmer of light coming from John's room. She hesitated, her courage almost failing her, then she moved silently towards his door. She opened it without knocking, and closed it softly behind her, her heart thumping in the darkness.

'Jack?' Hester whispered. 'Are you awake?'

A light snapped on beside the bed and John sat up, pushing the hair from his eyes, his face incredulous for a second before he recovered himself. He stared at her blankly.

'Something wrong with Jo?' he asked instantly.

'No.' Hester swallowed, and walked towards the bed, conscious of the bias-cut silk clinging to her breasts and hips. She could see the uneven rise and fall of John's bare chest, which belied the expressionless mask of his face, and somewhere deep inside her there was a surge of triumph.

'Is there something wrong?' he asked.

'No.' Hester smiled, her eyes uncertain in the soft light. 'I came to thank you for such a beautiful present.'

'I'm glad you're pleased.' His voice sounded uneven. 'One for work and one for pleasure.' His heavy lids failed to hide the fact that his eyes were drawn irresistibly to her breasts, which rose and fell rapidly to the rhythm of her breathing.

'And I came to say I'm sorry, Jack.' Hester came to a halt, almost at the edge of the bed. There was a pulse throbbing in his bare throat, plainly visible to her fascinated eye. She would have liked to put out a finger to touch it, but lacked the courage. For the moment.

'Sorry for what?' he asked softly.

'For constantly taking, I suppose, and never giving.' Her eyes dropped and she stood still. 'You have been unfailingly generous to me, ever since—well, what I mean is that all I've ever given you in return is Jo.'

'You don't make use of the money I allow you.'

Hester was in no mood to be side-tracked.

'I have a third reason for coming, Jack,' she said, before she could change her mind. 'If—if you still favour the idea, I've changed my mind about the platonic bit.'

John's body tensed, his eyes glittering as they stared into hers.

'Why?'

Hester made a quick decision. Half the truth was all she could manage.

'May I sit down, Jack? This is rather difficult for me.'

He closed his eyes for a split-second, then nodded.

'Please do. I can't get up to offer you a seat.'

Hester subsided on the foot of the bed, her head bowed and her hair falling forward to hide the hectic colour in her cheeks, wondering irrelevantly why she should feel so hot, when her nightgown was the scantiest one she'd ever owned.

'The other time,' she began, then stopped and looked

at him in appeal. 'I mean, the only—well, that night at Camilla's——'

'I get the drift,' he said quickly, his voice stifled.

'What I'm trying to say is that was it. My one and only brush with—with that sort of thing. Don't get angry, but it didn't exactly fill me with the urge to experiment further, especially when it turned out to be rather a case of crime and punishment, if you see what I mean.'

'I see very well,' he said flatly. 'My crime, your punishment.'

'No, no.' She dismissed this impatiently. 'What I'm trying to say is that I'm a bit nervous, Jack, that's all. Nothing personal. I liked the way you kissed me upstairs. You know that very well, it must have been patently obvious. But I've got cold feet about the rest of it.'

John sat up and reached forward, capturing her hands in his, the molten light back in his eyes. 'If you mean you came to share my bed, Hester, I shall welcome you quite literally with open arms. But if you just came to give me a clinical explanation then I suggest you get the hell out of here right now, while you can!'

Hester looked at him sharply, taken aback at the laughing violence in his voice, then saw the naked hunger burning in his eyes and got up as if jerked by a rope, stumbling forward into his outstretched arms.

'You're in Daddy's bed!' The voice was accusing, and Hester struggled to free herself from the arms that held her fast as she peered over the duvet at her indignant daughter, who was standing at the foot of the bed. She could feel the laughter shaking John's bare chest against her shoulder blades, and said apologetically.

'Mummies and Daddies usually share a bed, Jo.'

Jo regarded them both with unconcealed satisfaction.

'You didn't mind dis-disturbing Mummy this time then, Daddy!'

'No,' agreed John, in a rather unrecognisable voice. 'I didn't mind a bit.'

Hester quivered, biting her lip.

'Is it late, Baby?' she asked.

Jo shrugged her shoulders.

'Don't know. Denny's here. She just came.'

'Then why don't you put your dressing-gown on,' suggested John, sliding a hand over Hester's hip bone beneath the covers, 'and ask Denny to give you your breakfast, and we'll be up and dressed in five minutes.'

'O.K.' She slid off the bed to run to the door. 'Don't be long,' she ordered, and banged the door behind her.

Immediately John twisted Hester round in his arms and kissed her at such length, that for the first time since Jo's birth she wished her daughter were somewhere else, and she and John could simply stay where they were. Indefinitely. When he raised his head and looked lazily into her eyes he seemed to read her mind.

'I adore my darling daughter, but right at this moment I wish we'd come to some other arrangement about our honeymoon,' he said, brushing the tip of her nose with his lips. 'I have five years lost time to make up, Hester Ransome, and from my point of view at least I think we've made rather a good start.'

'I agree,' she said, so emphatically he laughed and kissed her again. Afterwards she lay looking at him. The face next to hers on the pillow seemed to have changed overnight. 'You look different,' she informed him.

'How?'

'You've lost that guarded, wary sort of look you always wear when I'm around.'

'Like a boxer anticipating a blow, if it's anything like I felt.' John gave her a little shake. 'You've led me quite a dance, Hester Ransome. Was it really worth it? Being married to me isn't so difficult really, is it?'

'It's far too early to commit myself,' said Hester primly. 'Will you get up first, please?'

He propped himself on one elbow and leered down at her.

'You're afraid that the sight of your naked body will inspire me to further excesses of lust, aren't you?'

'Yes. So have a look for my nightgown, then I'll get up.'

'How do I know whether the sight of *my* body won't send *you* berserk?' he demanded, and threw back the covers.

Hester gave a squeak and heaved herself over on her stomach, burying her face in the pillows. 'It's a chance you'll have to take,' she mumbled indistinctly.

'You don't have to play ostrich. I'm relatively decent—though God knows where your nightgown is.'

Hester sat up, clutching the duvet to her chest and pushed her tangled hair away from her eyes, to see John on his hands and knees on the floor, peering under the bed.

'You took it off,' she pointed out.

'I wasn't feeling tidy at the time.' He flung his head back to grin up at her. 'I just threw it somewhere.'

Hester giggled, and turned to fish around under the pillows, finally locating a crumpled ball of silk.

'Found it. Turn around, please, while I put it on.'

John sprang to his feet, laughing at her.

'Why? We are married, you goose.'

'Yes, I know. Twice! Nevertheless I need time to get used to it. Until now it's all been a matter of theory rather than practice—so go away.'

Obediently John turned his back while Hester slid into the nightgown and made for the door, only to be intercepted before she opened it.

'I wish you'd agreed to a honeymoon,' John said huskily, and slid his arms round her, tugging gently on her hair with one hand so that her throat was available to his mouth, which slid down it in a series of kisses that made Hester go weak at the knees.

'Please——' she gasped. 'I must get dressed—Jack, please!'

He let her go abruptly, his eyes glittering in triumph.

'Only for the moment, Mrs Ransome. See you at breakfast.'

It took Hester ages to shower and dress. She was all fingers and thumbs, and every now and then found herself staring absently into space, finally pulling herself together when Jo came running in with Scrap, demanding to wear her red dungarees to Auntie Cam's.

'Daddy says we're having lunch there,' she said excitedly.

Still in her slip Hester quickly helped Jo into her red-patterned white Norwegian sweater and the red dungarees, then she put on her own dress after the child had scampered away. Today she wanted to look as attractive as she could, unaware that there were new, dreamy lights in her eyes, and a warmth in her skin which had come into being overnight. She decided on a cream wool dress, by no means new, but one she knew very well was flattering. It was a stark little tube of a dress which took its shape from the curves beneath it, and for a touch of colour she added the jade beads given her by Lucy for a wedding present, then made up her face lightly and brushed her hair. Her eyes stared back at her from the mirror, brilliant and abstracted as she thought of the night before, unable to control the shortage of breath and dryness in her mouth at the memory.

'Aren't you ready, yet—I'm starving,' John said in her ear, almost startling her out of what wits she seemed to have left.

'Sorry,' she said breathlessly, and went to look for shoes in the wardrobe, emerging with the delicate high-heeled pumps worn the day before for the ceremony. 'Will these do?' She frowned at them critically and held them against her dress.

'Wear hob-nailed boots, as long as you get a move on,' he said unromantically, 'I could eat a horse.'

By coincidence John was dressed in similar colours to herself, with Aran sweater over a cream wool shirt and fawn tweed trousers.

'We could be brother and sister,' said Hester suddenly, as he pulled her up the stairs. 'We've both got longish faces and fair hair, and today even our colour schemes match.'

John came to a halt at the top of the stairs and stared down at her from beneath half-closed lids.

'After last night, Hester, I'm very happy with the idea of marriage as a passionate friendship. But a brother to you I am not, nor am I ever likely to be—now for pity's sake let's eat.'

CHAPTER EIGHT

THEIR breakfast together was a light-hearted affair, more worthy of the term 'wedding-breakfast' than the elaborate lunch of the day before. John Lauder Ransome, electronics tycoon, was totally transformed into someone else entirely, someone Hester felt she'd never met before. Mrs Denham beamed as she plied them both with grapefruit, grilled bacon and poached eggs, followed by wholewheat toast spread with marmalade apparently made by Camilla in one of her domesticated spasms.

'Do you realise, Hester, that I've never eaten anything you've cooked yet,' observed John, grinning at her. 'Do you serve soufflé glacé for breakfast and rum babas for lunch?'

'Only if I'm paid to do so,' she retorted. 'I *can* cook savoury dishes I assure you. Only when am I going to have the opportunity, Jack? I don't want to offend your Denny.'

'She'll gladly keep to the housework once you say the word—good plain cook is how she describes herself, so now I have the services of a beautiful one she can step down.' He helped himself to a third slice of toast and held out his cup for more coffee.

Hester looked at him sharply, to see if he were joking. Apparently he was not.

'I've never thought of myself as beautiful,' she said.

John shook his head in wonder.

'But I caught you gazing into the mirror just now. Surely you could see yourself.'

She gave a funny, embarrassed little laugh.

'I wasn't really looking.'

'I know you weren't. I watched you.' His voice deepened. 'What were you thinking about, Hester?'

Their sudden, shared look of intimacy sent the colour rushing into her face and she looked hurriedly away.

'You know perfectly well,' she said with difficulty.

He reached over and took her hand.

'Yes I do. I thought I was dreaming when you suddenly materialised in my bedroom last night.'

'It seemed only fair—'

'You mean you offered yourself as payment?' he demanded.

'No, no. But when you went to bed so suddenly I felt wretched, small.' Hester smiled at him ruefully. 'Suddenly it was all so simple. I can't think now why I made a fuss in the first place.'

'It wasn't the ordeal you anticipated, then,' he said, straight-faced.

'You could put it that way.' She smiled at him with a warmth that brought him out of his seat to kiss her, but he only had time to touch his mouth to hers before Jo came bouncing into the room, demanding when they were going to lunch with Auntie Cam.

'Not for a while, I hope,' said her mother breathlessly. 'We haven't finished breakfast yet.'

'You are slow! I wanted to wake you up early this morning, but Denny said no, 'cos you'd be tired.'

'Very true,' said John, his lips twitching as he looked across at his wife, who was suddenly very much occupied with clattering dishes together. 'You know, Hester, until now I'd never really believed in the blushing bride bit.'

'Neither had I,' said Hester tersely. 'I hope I tone down a bit before we get to Camilla's.' She looked at her daughter critically. 'I don't know that those dungarees are really a very good idea, Jo. Perhaps your new dress might be better.'

'Oh Mummy, no!' Jo scowled at the thought of changing her clothes again. John gave her a push.

'Go on, miss. Do as Mummy says. She's the boss.'

Hester gave him a glinting green look.

'May I have that in writing?'

'Any way you like,' he said, his face perfectly serious, and Hester retreated, inwardly confused, to button her daughter into her dress.

They were a little later than intended arriving at Camilla's, and to Hester's dismay there were several cars in the Desmond drive, as well as outside in the road.

'What the—' John bit back a curse, and reversed the Daimler back along the road to find a parking space. 'I thought this was to be a quiet family lunch.'

Hester's spirits plummeted. She glanced down at herself.

'I'm not dressed for anything special, Jack. I assumed it was just an opportunity to get to know your parents better.'

'So did I!' He smiled at her reassuringly. 'Not that you've anything to worry about—you look gorgeous.'

'And me, Daddy? Am I gorgeous too? demanded Jo.

'Absolutely.' He lifted her out of the car and gave her a pat on the bottom. 'I'm very lucky to have two such beautiful ladies to escort.' He took his daughter by the hand, put an arm round his wife's waist, and this was how Camilla found her three guests of honour when she flung open the door in welcome.

'Darlings, come in. I've sprung a little surprise party on you—don't be cross with me!'

Hester kissed Camilla's cheek and raised an eyebrow at the hubbub coming from the drawing room.

'Doesn't sound terribly little!'

'You are an ass, Cam,' said John with feeling. 'We weren't expecting a crush like this.'

'Rubbish! It's only the neighbours for a few drinks.' Camilla took Jo's hand. 'Come on, poppet—you're wearing that super dress again, I see. Let's say hello to Grannie and Grandad, then you can have a look for Nimrod and Jumble out in the garden. I think there's a surprise waiting for you out there, too.'

'Come on, Hester, let's get it over with.' John put a hand at the back of his wife's slender waist, and propelled her into Camilla's drawing-room, which at first glanced seemed jammed to capacity with wall-to-wall guests as they ran the gauntlet of introductions and congratulations on their way to join John's parents. When they finally made it Hester was glad to stay close by Delia Ransome's side while Camilla went on bringing up latecomers to be introduced and Mike Desmond kept their glasses filled with a very pale dry sherry he kept only for special guests, as he told Hester confidentially. He was a big, burly man, twenty years older than Camilla, and very solid and reassuring among the shifting mass of strangers.

'Camilla *would* invite all these people,' said Mrs Ransome in Hester's ear. 'I would have preferred a quiet lunch on our own, but she was determined to celebrate John's wedding in her own particular way.'

Hester smiled.

'Your daughter's a very kind lady. It's sweet of her to go to so much trouble. But if you'd like a quiet meal together before you go back perhaps I could cook dinner for you at Prospect one evening.'

'But Hester, it's your honeymoon.' Mrs Ransome noted the rush of colour in her new daughter-in-law's cheeks with approval.

'I can still cook a meal. I'd like to, really.'

John returned from the garden and slid an arm round Hester's waist.

'All right?' he asked.

'Fine. I was just suggesting that your parents—and Camilla and Mike, too, of course, came to dinner at Prospect. I'd like to cook a meal for them.'

He grinned down at her teasingly.

'Just to prove to me you can cook, I suppose.'

'Of course she can,' broke in Mike jovially, appearing like a genie, sherry bottle in hand. 'Jolly fine do she catered for right here. Don't you remember—'

Remembrance hit him painfully, and he went a ripe shade of plum as his mother-in-law speared him with an icy grey look.

Hester put a hand on his arm and smiled at him warmly.

'Nice of you to put in a good word for me, Mike. I'll be glad to try some of my favourite recipes out on you.'

'Humble pie?' suggested Mrs Ransome, and Mike withdrew hastily as she turned to Hester with a smile. 'Very graceful, my dear.'

'There's not much point in getting uptight about it,' said Hester frankly. 'We have a constant little reminder we brought with us, for one thing. Besides, I met quite a few of the people here on that fateful occasion.'

'If only my plane had been on time that night we would probably have avoided a great deal of trouble, one way and another,' said John, suddenly grave as his eyes rested on Hester's face. She felt chilled. Was that how he thought of their marriage in his heart of hearts—as an accident that need never have happened? Someone attracted John's attention and pulled him away at that moment, and he missed the shadow that dimmed her earlier luminosity, and with keen perception her new mother-in-law began to talk of the day before, and what a charming little wedding it had been.

'Pity your mother couldn't make it today.' agreed Mr Ransome. 'Damned pretty woman. Said she had some lunch on with her bridge club.'

'Yes,' said Hester, firmly closing her mind on her misgivings. 'The club has its annual Christmas luncheon early, so Mother's gone off with Mrs Drayton to eat unseasonal turkey and Christmas pudding, then play in a light-hearted tournament.'

'Never mastered the game myself,' said Mrs Ransome. 'Do you play, Hester?'

'No. I'm not really a card-player——'

'Chess is more to her taste,' put in John, who rejoined them at that moment.

'Too slow for me,' objected his father. 'Can't stand all that mooning about for hours before making a move. Give me a round of golf any time.'

'Do you play chess much, Hester?' asked Mrs Ransome.

'She's been playing for years,' put in John, before Hester could say anything. 'It's just one of the things we both enjoy doing together.'

Hester smiled and excused herself.

'I think I'll just go and see what Jo's doing for a moment. She must be cold.'

She made her way through the crowded room, stopping to talk here and there as various friendly neighbours of Camilla's exchanged a word or two. As Hester made her escape through the kitchen she smiled wryly. Not too many bridges came complete with five year old child, a subject on which all Camilla's friends were being determinedly tactful. Hester had some trouble in locating Jo in the large, rambling garden, which had a paddock out of sight of the house, where she finally ran Jo to earth after a moment's instinctive anxiety. The child had mud on her duffel coat and tears in her eyes as she looked up into one of the trees at the end of the field, with Bundle the dog barking and leaping around at the trunk.

Hester tore through the long grass, to the detriment of her high, slender heels. 'What's the matter, Jo?' she called.

'It's my new kite,' cried the little girl in tearful distress. 'Uncle Mike bought it for me. It's a present, and Daddy showed me how to fly it, but he went back in to you and now it's stuck up in the tree.'

The gaily coloured kite was well and truly entangled in the top branches of the tree, its beribboned tail fluttering in the breeze, eluding Hester's hands as she tried to catch it. When she finally grabbed hold of the string and pulled nothing happened. The kite was firmly lodged, it seemed. Hester sighed, and cast a look over her shoulder, but no one was in sight, and just then a gust of wind threatened to whip the kite away altogether.

'Mummy, Mummy,' screamed Jo. 'It's blowing away!'

'Oh for heaven's sake,' said Hester impatiently, and kicked off her shoes. 'Here, take care of these.' Jo watched in tearful admiration as Hester sprang for the first branch and swung herself up until she had a good foothold, then edged herself slowly into a position of reasonable safety where she could assess how far she needed to climb before she could reach the kite. Very gingerly she hauled herself slowly up to the next branch, praying no one would appear to see her making such a cake of herself, and bit by bit she managed to crawl and heave herself up the tree until she was within reach of the kite. She cast a quick look down at Jo, and regretted it immediately as a wave of giddiness gripped her and the branches did a quick dance in front of her eyes. She closed them, forced to wait until the world steadied itself again.

'Up a bit higher, Mummy,' Jo called.

'The things I do for you, Josephine Ransome,' muttered Hester, and made a last superhuman effort to reach the kite, managing to dislodge it by stretching her arm to the utmost.

'Hester—for God's sake what are you doing!' John's irate bellow distracted her attention right at the crucial moment. There was an ominous creaking noise and Hester, plus branch, came crashing down, her fall only partly broken by John's body as he hurled himself forward to catch her. They ended in an ignominious heap, tangled together and partially winded, to the accompaniment of terrified screams from Jo, and the comforting tones of an attractive, husky voice trying to calm her down.

'There, there, darling, they're perfectly all right. See—your Mummy's getting up now.'

'Are you all right, Hester?' John hauled her to her feet, breathing hard. 'What the hell were you doing up a tree?'

Hester was too short of breath to do anything but point and gasp 'Kite!'

'Where?'

'Up in the sky,' wailed Jo. 'It's gone. I'm sorry, Mummy, I made you go up the tree.' She hurled herself into Hester's arms, sobbing against her mother in an agony of remorse.

'Hey!' remonstrated Hester breathlessly. 'Come on! I'm fine. I don't know about Daddy, though. I fell right on top of him.'

'Like a ton of bricks,' groaned John, and detached Jo from Hester to mop her face, his eyes anxious as they looked Hester up and down. 'Are you really all in one piece? Not just putting a brave face on it?'

'No, really, Jack. I'm just sorry the kite got away though, after all that.'

'To blazes with the kite—oh sorry, Jo.' John patted her head. 'Don't worry, we'll get you another one.' Suddenly he recollected himself, and turned to the young woman standing a little distance away, watching the scene with detached enjoyment. She held out Hester's shoes.

'These must be yours, Mrs Ransome.'

Hester met the bright amusement in dark eyes that were instantly familiar beneath the cap of glossy black hair. Five years had made little difference to the impact of Laura Verney's looks.

'Of course you two haven't met,' said John, picking up a very subdued Jo. 'Hester, this is Laura Browning, who used to work with me. Laura, my wife, Hester.'

'How do you do Mrs Browning.' Hester avoided shaking hands by accepting her shoes with a polite smile. She slid them on her damp feet, conscious of untidy hair, not to mention the fine coating of leaves and twigs which had attached themselves lovingly to the fine wool of her dress.

Laura responded with a sparkling, white-toothed smile.

'I'm so pleased to meet you at last. I'm afraid I'm a gate-crasher, but I was passing by Prospect and called in on impulse, so when darling old Denny said you were all here at Mrs Desmond's I felt I couldn't leave the neighbourhood without popping in for a few minutes.'

'How very nice of you,' said Hester serenely. 'Do come back to the house and have a drink while I rid myself of some of the great outdoors. Come, Jo. Let's have a wash—neither of us is fit for polite company.'

'Don't be long, Hester,' said John, setting Jo on her feet. His eyes narrowed as they rested on Hester's face for a moment. 'It's damned cold out here, you must both be frozen.' He walked them back briskly through the garden and into the house.

'In all the excitement I hardly noticed the cold,' said Hester lightly, and shepherded Jo off to the cloakroom in the hall while John took Laura to join the guests. Hester washed Jo's face and dusted the dried mud from her coat and took it off, then shooed the child into the hall.

'Go and find Granny Ransome or Daddy, Baby. I need to tidy myself up.'

'Are you all right, Mummy? Truly?' Jo's face was very anxious.

'The only thing damaged was my dignity.' Hester smiled, and Jo ran off reassured, as Camilla emerged from the kitchen, obviously distraught.

'Could I go up to your room, Camilla? I'm an absolute mess!' Hester gave her a cheerful grin.

'Of course, darling. Lord! What on earth have you been doing?' She took Hester by the arm and hurried her upstairs, hissing, 'and what on earth is Laura doing here?'

In Camilla's bedroom Hester accepted a clothes brush, shrugging.

'*I've* been climbing trees, but as far as Laura's concerned I've no idea.' She brushed vigorously at her dress and handed the brush to Camilla. 'Will you have a go at the back? She said she just happened to be passing Prospect.'

Camilla snorted.

'When you consider Prospect lies at the end of an unadopted road miles from anywhere that's a bit rich!'

'Could you lend me a comb and some lipstick, Camilla? My bag is downstairs.'

'Anything you want, darling, help yourself.' Camilla stepped back and viewed Hester's dress, frowning. 'It's all off now, I think. Why all the grass and stuff?'

'I not only climbed the tree, I fell out of it—no time to explain, now, I want to get back down there.'

They hurried down to the drawing-room where Laura was easy to pick out, despite the crush. For one thing she was wearing something which was possibly a designer track suit in sapphire blue velvet, and for another, as far as Hester was concerned, she was about as close to John as it was possible to be without actually being in his arms. John turned as Hester came toward him, his eyes lighting up as he saw her, a fact which Mrs Browning noted and filed for future reference, as Hester could see.

'Come and have a drink, Hester,' he said, holding out a hand. 'After the shock I sustained from having you land on top of me I gratefully accepted a brandy from Mike.'

Hester found herself the centre of an amused circle who teased her unmercifully about her tree-climbing.

'Why didn't you wait for help to arrive?' asked Laura, flashing a look around the assembled company. 'Plenty of muscles around here, as far as I can see.'

'The wind was getting up, and Jo was getting uptight,' said Hester. 'I'm afraid I couldn't resist her entreaties. Pretty futile, as it turned out, as we lost the kite after all my efforts.'

'Don't do anything like that again,' said John sternly. 'My nerves aren't up to it.'

Mike handed Hester a brandy.

'Straight down the hatch, sweetheart,' he advised. 'Best thing for shock.'

'I think Jack is the one suffering most from shock,' he laughed. 'I crash-landed on top of him.'

'Good thing you're so skinny,' said Laura sweetly.

Hester downed her drink and blinked a little, then let her eyes linger on the other woman's opulent, velvet-covered curves before meeting Laura's bright gaze head on. She nodded her head pleasantly.

'I've always had a weight problem—too. But mine is keeping it on rather than taking it off.' Hester smiled radiantly, then turned away to speak to Mrs Ransome, who was sitting in an armchair with Jo on her lap, lips twitching.

'I didn't realise you had claws, Hester,' she said in an undertone.

'Neither did I.' Hester made a face and put down the brandy glass. 'It's the alcohol. I should avoid it.'

'Had you never met Laura before?' asked Delia Ransome with interest.

'No. I'd only read about her in the article they did on Jack in one of the Sunday supplements. Is her husband here? I don't see anyone in the offing.'

'From what she said earlier I gather she's getting a divorce.'

Hester's spirits nose-dived even further.

'Perhaps she's after her old job.'

Jo raised a sleepy head from her grandmother's shoulder.

'I'm hungry, Mummy.'

Mrs Ransome patted her comfortingly.

'People are beginning to leave now, darling. We'll soon have lunch.'

It took some time for all the guests to make their goodbyes, until finally Laura Browning was the only one left, apart from the family. She stayed for what seemed like hours to Hester, apparently engrossed in a private conversation with John while Mike Desmond and Mr Ransome strolled in the garden smoking pipes, and Camilla went pointedly back and forth to the kitchen several times. At long last Laura turned to Hester and held out her hand, and this time Hester had no option but to take it.

'It's been so good to meet you at last—I had no idea you and John had remarried, you know. When did all this happen?'

'Yesterday,' said Hester briefly, and disengaged her hand.

Laura's enamelled poise slipped a little.

'Yesterday?' She looked at John and gave an odd little laugh. 'Goodness, I had no idea you were a *new* bride, Hester. After all, you can hardly count the first time.'

'No, I don't,' agreed Hester woodenly.

'No honeymoon?' Laura's gaze flicked from John's face to Hester's, and he moved casually to slide an arm round Hester's waist.

'We're saving that for later on,' he said, and brushed his lips against Hester's curls. 'For the moment we're merely spending a quiet week at Prospect.'

Laura's eyes slid over to Jo, cuddled on Mr Ransome's lap.

'And baby makes three,' she said with a little laugh. 'Well, I mustn't outstay my welcome.' She bade fulsome goodbyes to everyone, including an embarrassingly hostile Camilla, who showed her to the door with ill concealed relief.

'What's she doing here, John?' she demanded, when they were finally seated at the dining table. 'I thought she hailed from down south somewhere.'

'She's staying with friends in Oxford, I believe.'

'I think the young woman hoped to be asked to

lunch,' said Mr Ransome.

'She is an old friend, Father,' said John mildly, and helped Jo cut up her meat.

'Not of mine, she isn't.' Camilla shot a look at Hester, who was silently eating roast beef with an air of abstraction. 'Are you all right, Hester? Your tumble hasn't shaken you up?'

'No, not in the slightest.' Hester went on eating calmly, avoiding John's look.

'Well it did me,' he said emphatically. 'Damn well scared the living daylights out of me when I saw you balanced on one foot on a mere twig.'

'It was a perfectly sturdy branch,' she contradicted, 'and if you had kept quiet I'd never have fallen.'

'And the kite blew away,' said Jo dejectedly.

'Never mind, poppet,' consoled Mike. 'I'll get you another just like it, promise.'

It was late when they left the Desmonds. Jo fell asleep as soon as John started up the car, which gave Hester an excuse not to talk on the journey home, her mind simmering with the unexpected appearance of Laura. After one or two attempts at conversation John gave up, and they arrived at the house in silence, Jo fast asleep on her father's shoulder. Mrs Denham had drawn curtains and left lights on, and the house was pleasantly warm, Scrap rushing from the kitchen to welcome them. Hester managed to quiet her down without waking Jo, and let the dog out through the kitchen door for a run in the garden while John carried Jo downstairs and laid her on her bed.

'What shall we do about undressing her?' he asked Hester when she joined him.

'I doubt if she'll stir. She's very tired. You lift her a little and I'll slide her clothes off.'

Silently they worked together until Jo was tucked up in bed and the faithful little dog installed in her basket alongside the bed. Upstairs in the living-room the Sunday papers were neatly laid out on the table between the couches, and John stooped to put a match to the ready-laid fire.

'Is it worth it?' asked Hester. 'It's quite warm in here, and it's late. You might as well leave it for tomorrow.'

'As you like.' John straightened and looked at her, frowning a little. 'Would you like a drink, or tea?'

'No, nothing, thank you.' Hester avoided his eyes and sat down. 'I'll just have a browse through the Sunday papers, and then I think I'll have a bath.'

'Fine. Would you like some music?'

'Not particularly.' Hester was in no mood for a romantic background.

His mouth tightening, John sat down opposite and picked up one of the papers. There was silence in the room, broken only by the rustle of the newsheets, but it was an uncomfortable silence, all the rapport of the morning dissipated as though the events of the night before had never occurred. After a while Hester found it intolerable and she got up, needing to be alone.

'I'm off to have a bath, then,' she said casually.

'Right,' said John, without looking up.

Hester went downstairs and ran a bath, feeling tense and unhappy, her mind full of Laura Browning. The woman had been unconsciously instrumental in wrecking things the first time, admittedly, but now it looked as though she might have a shot at it in earnest. Certainly her timing was impeccable. Hester lay for a long time in the warm, perfumed water, too lack-lustre to read, trying hard to relax and keep her mind a blank, which was tricky, when all the time she was wondering what to do next, what she was expected to do next, and most important of all, what Jack was likely to do next.

Hester got out of the water at last, dried herself and put on a fresh nightgown, crisp lawn this time, in contrast to the thirties allure of the night before. She had a peep at Jo, who was dead to the world, then went to look at the bed in the room next door. If she slept in that Jack would probably consider it a slap in the face, but to walk the length of the hall and climb into bed in cold blood was utterly beyond her. Hester pondered unhappily, twisting a handful of hair round and round in her fingers as she wrestled with the dilemma.

'Problems?' John appeared in the doorway in his white robe, his thumbs hooked into the belt as he looked at her in enquiry.

'Yes.' Hester faced him candidly. 'I didn't know what to do, Jack. What you'd expect.'

'I don't *expect* anything, Hester.' His tone was lazily amused, and stung.

'That solves my problem, then,' she said flatly, and turned back her duvet.

'Good night.'

'Not so fast.' He moved like lightening from the door and caught her wrist. 'I said I didn't expect, Hester. Which doesn't mean I don't hope, or want, to have you share my bed. There was no opportunity to talk this morning, as we should have while you were still warm and receptive, and now you've slipped away from me again.' Slowly he pulled her towards him, inch by inch, until she was held close against him. 'What's wrong, Hester?' he whispered into her hair. 'Tell me what's troubling you.'

Hester stayed ram-rod still in his embrace. Surely he must know what was the matter. It was Laura, with her Lone Ranger drawl and proprietary manner towards her former employer, or associate, or lover, or however she thought of John Lauder Ransome in her highly informed mind. Hester tried to free herself, finding it hard to breathe.

'Nothing's troubling me,' she said in a dead little voice.

'Then in that case . . .' John switched off the lamp and picked her up as if she were Jo, taking her along the hall to his own room, which was dark. He kicked the door shut, dumped Hester on the bed, got rid of his robe and got in beside her, pulling her tightly against him.

'Tomorrow you move your belongings in here with me,' he said tersely. 'Then you'll have no problems other than how best to please your husband. And now I intend to remove all doubts on that score also, by showing you precisely how.'

Hester struggled violently against the hands that removed her nightgown, but she subsided abruptly as he said in an unfamiliar, harsh tone,

'Enough Hester. You began this. If you had kept to your own bed last night I would have respected the decision, kept to the promise I made you of no demands. But you chose to come to me, and that established a precedent. I want you here where you are now, tonight, tomorrow night and every night in the future. I'm not asking if you agree, because I'm pretty damned sure you don't, but I want to know you understand. I'm not precisely sure what turned a warm, responsive bride back into an iceberg again, but whatever it is won't make a blind bit of difference. You may not love me, or even like me very much, but you're bloody well going to co-habit with me, in every sense of the word.'

Hester braced herself for a violence which never happened. The night before John's manner had been one of disbelief, his treatment of her almost reverent, but this time he set out deliberately to demonstrate exactly how much sensation she was capable of feeling, using consummate skill to set her every nerve end alight and tingling in anticipation of the rapture he brought her to not once, but several times before his body joined hers in a wild culmination of pleasure, his face above her almost austere in its sexual demand.

It was daylight when she woke fully. A wintry, pale sunlight showed through the filmy white curtains veiling the window which made up one entire wall of the room. The inner corded silk curtains were drawn back to give a view of the garden and shrubbery far below, where Hester could see Jo running with the dog, John's tall, athletic figure in pursuit. She rubbed her eyes, then lay still, the events of the night coming back to her in a flood. She frowned as she thought of his trenchant little lecture before he began to make love to her. He had been very lucid, with no possibility of misunderstanding. Now she knew very clearly what her marriage was to entail, and she might just as well get out of bed and get on with the every day side of it as well as the every night.

Hester was taken aback to find it was gone mid-day when she came out of the shower, and hastily threw on slacks and sweater, frowning at her face as she splashed cold water on heavy eyes and tried to disguise swollen lips with a touch of lipstick. All the tell-tale signs were there for anyone who cared to look, and Hester hoped Mrs Denham was not of an observant nature in such matters. Happily the lady was nowhere to be seen and the house was deserted, though a fire burned in the living room, and everywhere was spick and span, as usual. Hester made herself a pot of tea, and drank it almost dry before Jo burst in from the garden, her face glowing, followed at a more leisurely pace by her father.

'Mummy! Are you better? Daddy said I mustn't disturb you.' Jo was obviously very proud of this new word, and Hester laughed, hugging the little figure to her.

'I'm fine, Baby. What have you been doing?'

'Playing ball. And now Daddy's going to play Ludo with me.' Jo ran to take her anorak off and Hester looked up at John uncertainly. He smiled briskly.

'Morning, Hester. Mrs Denham's having a day off today, so what do you propose for lunch?'

'Good morning,' said Hester faintly, then rallied. 'I don't know. I'll inspect the basic ingredients available and see what I can do. Sorry to be so lazy—you should have woken me, but I shan't be too long getting a meal together.'

'Good girl.' He patted her shoulder in friendly

fashion and went off to join Jo, looking fit and healthy
in a grey track suit and trainers, his thick, blond hair
windblown, and a fresh colour in his lean face. Hester
was lost for words. She had known that the euphoric
atmosphere of previous morning was unlikely, but after
the undreamed of the intimacies of the night Jack's
brisk impersonal friendliness seemed incongruous. It
was like spending the night with Don Juan and waking
up with the sportsmaster. Hester shrugged, and had a
look through the refrigerator, which yielded up salad
ingredients, most dairy products, and plastic containers
of bacon and sausages.

It was the work of moments to find flour in one of
the cupboards and make pastry while the oven heated.
Hester baked two quiche bases 'blind', then filled one
with cooked bacon, tomatoes, cheese and eggs, and the
other with leeks, mushrooms and peppers in a cheese
sauce. She rubbed a salad bowl with garlic then tossed
lettuce, cress and cucumber in it with oil and vinegar,
and put two sausages in the oven for Jo in case she was
in one of her unadventurous moods. While the quiches
baked she set the kitchen table for three, sliced
wholewheat bread and put coffee to percolate, then
whipped Mrs Denham's apron off as the timer signalled
everything was ready. Hester put the quiches on the
table, then strolled across the hall to the living-room.

'Lunch,' she said casually, and held out her hand to
Jo. 'Come and wash your hands.'

John was very complimentary about the hastily
prepared meal and ate hugely, which inspired Jo to
follow suit, eating not only her sausages but a slice of
the bacon quiche and most of her salad. Hester was
hungry too. Far more than usual, and for reasons
which embarrassed her to remember. Having lunch in
the kitchen was fun, and she enjoyed the domestic
atmosphere with a husband who was matter-of-fact and
friendly and even brought up a rather fraught topic
without the slightest trace of constraint.

'Have you moved your things yet, Hester?' His eyes were direct, and entirely without innuendo.

'No, not yet,' Hester replied in kind. 'I've been disgustingly lazy this morning, but I'll get on with it after lunch.'

'Don't be long, then, as I thought we'd take Scrap for a walk this afternoon,' he suggested, 'take advantage of the sunshine.'

And so the day passed, in activities just like any family who had lived together in the normal way for years, instead of this brand-new three-sided partnership. While they strolled along the footpath that wound through the fields beyond the house Hester asked John if he minded Alicia's name being added to the guest list for the family dinner party.

'Good God, no.' John paused to look at her in surprise. 'Why should I mind?'

'Well, the idea was to have more time to spend with your parents, strictly speaking.' Hester threw her scarf back round her neck to keep out the chill breeze and took firmer hold of Scrap's leash. 'You've already spent quite a lot of time with *my* mother, unknown to me.'

'And will happily spend more.' John took her arm and they strolled on after Jo. 'Besides, you're concerned about her feeling lonely, I know.'

'Yes, I am. It would be pretty odd if she weren't, really.'

John nodded sympathetically, then grinned down at her.

'She was certainly a hit with my father, you know. Always had a weakness for blondes, the old man. I imagine your mother was very pretty when she was younger.'

'She was.' Hester gave him a mischievous little look. 'I take after my father.'

He stopped and turned her to face him.

'Pretty is not the right word for you. As I've told you before, you're beautiful.' His voice was anything but impersonal for a moment, and Hester's breath caught.

'Thank you, kind sir,' she said, deliberately flippant. 'I'd describe myself as an acquired taste.'

'I've had long enough to acquire it, God knows.' John dropped her hand and raced down the path towards Jo, who had gone on too far ahead. 'Hang on, pet, there's a stream down there. Wait for me.'

Scrap barked excitedly and pulled Hester after the others, giving her no time to dwell on his words as John carefully guided first Jo, then herself, over the stepping-stones in the stream.

Later that evening, after Jo was in bed, Hester brought up the subject of menus, and asked John about his likes and dislikes in the way of food.

'No kidneys, or brains, please,' he asked with a shudder, 'or any animal spare parts like that, but otherwise practically anything. I like fish very much. So do my parents, by the way, and I know Camilla prefers Mike to keep off duck, if that's any help for your dinner party. You realise, though, that my entire family is likely to expect something fairly spectacular in the way of dessert?'

'I know. To be honest I'm a bit nervous, Jack.' Hester made a face. 'Silly isn't it, when I've earned my living by cooking for special occasions.' She gave a nervous little yawn, and rubbed her eyes.

'Whatever you do will be a success, if today's offerings were anything to go by, so don't worry about it.' John sprang to his feet. 'Up you come. Bed.'

'But it's early yet——'

'You look tired. No more protests. Come on.' John was implacable, and Hester found herself in bed almost before she knew what was happening. She held her breath as John slid in beside her, but he merely gave her a brisk kiss on her cheek, turned her in his arms so that she lay with her back curved into his body, and with a brief good-night settled himself for sleep. Hester lay still, tense with surprise as much as anything else, then gradually relaxed, soothed by the sound of John's deep, even breathing, liking the security of strong arms holding her close.

Without Hester realising it a pattern for her marriage had been established. The days passed in easy, friendly companionship, she and John getting to know each other better, learning to be mutual parents to their child and just generally getting accustomed to being a family. The nights were something else. Hester never knew whether her bedfellow was likely to be a nocturnal extension of her daytime companion or a demanding, exciting lover who gave, and expected in return, the ultimate in sexual satisfaction. The uncertainty added an edge, a seasoning of spice, to the pleasant daily routine that soon became a habit. The dinner-party took place at the end of the week, and was a great success, not only because the food Hester served was delicious, but because everyone so plainly enjoyed themselves, Alicia particularly.

'You look well, Hester,' she said, when they were alone for a moment in the kitchen.

'I am.' Hester smiled at her mother steadily and Alicia nodded, reassured.

'So your marriage isn't quite the terrible penance you seemed to imagine it would be,' she said drily.

Hester wrinkled her nose at her, laughing.

'No. It isn't. John and I get along fairly well, all things considered. Jo, of course, is in seventh heaven, as you saw for yourself, and really the only thing bothering me is what I'm going to do with my time when John's back at the saltmines and Jo goes back to school after half-term.'

'How about a good rest?' suggested Alicia. 'You've been driving yourself very hard these past few years; a spot of slacking might be a good idea—sheer idleness for a change.'

Hester shook her head emphatically.

'Not my scene. I can't endure the thought of it.'

'Girlish confidences?' John's voice sounded cold as he interrupted them to get ice from the fridge.

'I was just telling Hester how well she looked,' said Alicia quickly.

John's face was hidden as he opened the fridge door and rummaged in the freezer compartment. 'All the exercise and fresh air she's getting, Alicia.' He smiled as he emerged. 'Dad is demanding your presence loudly—good thing my mother's not the jealous type.'

'Really, John!' Alicia laughed, but cast a doubtful look at Hester and John as she left them together.

John stared down into Hester's face in the bright revealing light.

'What can't you endure, Hester? This——?' He seized her and kissed her hard, opening her lips with his tongue and pulling her hips close against him, one hand straying over the clinging silk that covered her breasts before sliding inside to seek nipples that sprang to life at his touch. 'Well?' he demanded in a hoarse whisper, 'Is it this you can't stand—or this? If so, you're lying. Your body tells me a different story——'

Hester tried to explain, but his mouth cut off her words and she gave up, letting him do just as he, and she, wanted, until they were interrupted by an embarrassed cough from the doorway.

'Frightfully sorry,' said Camilla awkwardly, 'but Mother would like a glass of fruit juice.'

Hester broke away from John, her cheeks scarlet, and hurried to take a carton of orange juice from the fridge and pour some into a glass.

'Only to be expected,' John told his sister, unembarrassed. 'We *are* on our honeymoon.'

Camilla gave a loud giggle and took the glass from Hester.

'Oh don't mind me, darlings—I'll leave you to it. Just take up where you left off!'

She hurried back to the others and John eyed Hester with a very explicit look.

'We'll do just that later on, Hester, in private. In the meantime we'd better get back to the party.'

'You can. I'll just tidy myself up and have a look in on Jo,' she said with dignity, and went downstairs to put herself back together again, still quivering inwardly from John's onslaught, and not at all sure she cared for the hint of menace in his promise of deferment.

It was a very convivial evening. Hester put the incident in the kitchen from her mind, and recounted some of the more amusing incidents of her catering career, to John's surprise, his eyes never leaving her face as she talked. It was the last night before the senior Ransomes' return to their home in the Algarve, to the restored farmhouse near Silves where they now lived.

'Very quiet and not at all fashionable,' said Delia Ransome, 'but we like it. You must bring Hester and Jo out for a holiday, John.'

'I shall do next summer, Mother. Pity you won't be here for Christmas, but I suppose Dad's chest will object if you stay in England in midwinter.' John gave his father a sympathetic smile.

'Not to mention the arthritis,' agreed Mrs Ransome, and turned to Alicia. 'Don't suppose you get troubled with such things at your age, Mrs Price?'

'Don't you believe it,' she laughed. 'Besides, I'm no spring chicken, you know!'

'Nonsense,' he declared gallantly. 'A mere slip of a thing compared with us old stagers, eh Delia?'

His wife raised her elegantly coiffeured grey head and looked at him in amused exasperation. 'I agree in principle, Edward, but can't help feeling you might have put it more gracefully.'

There was general laughter, and the party broke up soon after, as the Ransomes had seats on a charter flight from Birmingham International the following morning.

As Delia Ransome kissed Hester's cheek she said softly, 'Be happy, my dear. Not just for your child's sake, but your own. Try to put the past where it belongs—in the past.'

Alicia went with the others, in Mike Desmond's car, and the house was quiet as Hester tidied up, filling the dishwasher and putting food in containers while John cleared the big living room of glasses and canapé dishes.

'The meal was superb, Hester,' he said as he brought a loaded tray into the kitchen. 'Most impressive.'

'I'm glad you were pleased.' Hester felt a glow at his praise. 'I had to curb the urge to show off, I must confess. In the end I kept it fairly simple—not much point in a complicated meal with the hostess rushing in and out of the kitchen like a maniac. Denny was a tremendous help beforehand, of course.'

'Why didn't you let her stay to wash up? She would have.' John leaned against a counter, arms folded, watching Hester as she moved swiftly to and fro, methodically reducing the kitchen to order.

'She does have a family of her own to see to, Jack. I felt guilty about keeping her so late as it was.' Hester carefully covered the chocolate pear flan with film and stored the tangerine sorbet in a polythene container.

'What were those things you served with the sorbet?' asked John.

'Lychees—and almonds, of course. Did you like the Provençal fish salad we had for a starter, by the way? You said your parents liked fish.'

'It was outstanding—so was the Rocquefort butter with the steaks, *and* everything else.' John caught her hand as she passed and turned her towards him. 'Thank you, Hester.' He stared down very intently into her clear green eyes. 'It's a week now. Do you think you'll survive being married?'

Her eyes remained steady.

'Yes, Jack. I'll survive.'

There was no definable change in his expression, nevertheless Hester could tell her answer was not the one he wanted. They remained as they were for a moment when suddenly Hester jumped violently as a scream of anguish came up from downstairs, accompanied by the dog's whimpering. With a muffled exclamation John sprinted across the hall and leapt down the stairs, Hester close behind him. Jo sat bolt upright in her bed, her eyes wide and staring, her hands straight out in front of her as if she were warding something, or someone, off. Scrap was on her hind legs, her front paws on the bed, making little sounds of distress.

John swept the child up in his arms, but she struggled and kicked, screaming as he tried to hold her close.

'She's not fully awake, Jack,' warned Hester and sat on the bed, holding out her arms. 'Give her to me.'

Breathing hard, his face ashen, John delivered his hysterical child into her mother's arms, the little body quietening instantly as it came into contact with Hester, who rocked back and fore, murmuring unintelligible comfort into the small ear until Jo was calm. The terrified green eyes returned to normal in the blotchy, damp little face and Jo went limp, burying her face against her mother's shoulder. John stood like someone turned to stone, pain in his eyes as he stared down at Jo. Hester's attention shifted from her child, and she smiled reassuringly as she looked up at him.

'She didn't know you, Jack.'

At the sound of her mother's voice Jo stirred and sat up, rubbing her knuckles in her eyes, then looked up, still sobbing dryly, and caught sight of John. Her face lit up and she stretched up her arms to him.

'Daddy!'

The relief on John's face made Hester's throat thicken in sympathy.

'Hey,' he said lightly, picking her up. 'What was all the fuss about?'

'Was it a dream?' she asked fearfully.

'That's right. Just a bad dream. All over now.'

'The man came—the blanket——' Jo shuddered and clutched John tightly.

'It was only a dream,' stressed Hester calmly. 'No man can get at you here, Jo, nor anywhere else.'

Jo's face brightened.

'He doesn't know I live here now, does he? Or where my school is.'

'No,' agreed John. 'You are perfectly safe, Jo. I promise.'

She yawned and snuggled against him.

'Will you read me a story?'

John looked at Hester, eyebrows raised, and she nodded.

'Just a little one then, darling,' he said. 'And then you must go straight to sleep.'

She nodded drowsily and let herself be tucked up in bed.

'I'll let poor old Scrap out,' said Hester, and left John sitting on Jo's bed while she went upstairs with the dog and waited at the kitchen door for her to come back. Jo was already asleep when Hester went down again, and after waiting for Scrap to settle herself down they backed quietly from the room and went along the hall to theirs. Hester slumped on the bed.

'I thought she was over it, Jack.'

He sat beside her and put an arm round her waist.

'These things probably take time, Hester. All we can do is give her plenty of love and security.' A tremor ran through him. 'My God, it was shattering when she fought me off!'

'She thought you were part of her dream, Jack. It was different with me, I'm female and familiar, and she knows my scent, I suppose.'

'So do I,' he said huskily, and at once the mood was different. Their emotions, brought to an unbearable pitch a few moments before, suddenly veered from anxiety to desire in the space of a heartbeat, and they were in each other's arms with an involuntary urge for physical comfort. All her senses honed by the recent shock, Hester felt John's hands on her skin with heightened perception, as if her skin were hyper-sensitive and his fingers endowed with different impulses that woke new responses everywhere he touched.

'Hester,' he groaned, and pulled her beneath him, his arousal instant and complete, so intense it was agony to delay the moments needed to free her body from her clothes and then tear off his own. For the first time there were no preliminary caresses. They came together in a fusion over which neither had any control until it had raged to its culmination, and left them exhausted and speechless in each other's arms. Hester fell asleep instantly, John's head on her breast, waking only once when he moved to his own side of the bed, taking her with him and holding her close against him as they slept again. She opened her eyes to daylight, to find John looking at her, propped on one elbow, watching her wake.

'Good morning,' he said quietly, and smiled.

Hester's heart turned over and she shut her eyes tightly to hide their expression, pretending to stretch and yawn.

'Good morning, Jack. Is it late?'

'No. Jo's fast asleep and Denny's not due for another hour.' He stayed where he was, not moving a muscle, and Hester's heart began to pound thickly.

'Shall we get up then?' she asked.

'If you want to. Do you?'

'Not particularly.'

'You don't care one way or another?'

Oh yes I care, she said silently, her eyes openly fierce on his. It's you who stays cool, Jack Ransome.

He frowned, and put out a finger to stroke her forehead.

'What is it? What have I done?'

'Nothing.'

'Is my lack of action the problem?' he asked softly.

Hester said nothing, but something in her eyes flashed a challenge that he took up with such intensity she forgot everything but the physical sensations sweeping over her like a spring tide.

CHAPTER NINE

HESTER was at a loose end. The house shone, the garden was subdued into winter tidiness, Jo was in school and John was away in Edinburgh. Christmas was only two weeks away and Hester had already made two large cakes, several puddings and a generous quantity of mincemeat. Even the shopping for presents was almost finished, in complete contrast to her former Christmas preparations, which had been a wild rush at the last minute, or done in odd moments left over from the frantic pre-festivity rush for the hotel. Today was Alicia's day at upholstery class, Jo was going straight from school to a birthday party, and Camilla was on a brief visit to her parents in Portugal. Everyone, it seemed, had something to do except Hester. She sighed and looked at her watch. Three o'clock. Hours to go before picking up Jo. She stood staring out at the view, which was beautiful even in its wintry greyness, but so still, nothing moving anywhere. She turned away restlessly, almost tripping over Scrap, who was sensitive to her mood and kept following her round the house, offering mute sympathy.

'The thing is, Scrap,' explained Hester, smoothing the dog's head, 'I'm not used to all this leisure. I just don't see myself as a pillar of the local W.I., or going to pottery classes, either. Don't breathe a word, but what I'd really like is another baby, but not as things are. If I were sure how Jack felt it would be different. Mind you, I think he does care for me, but I'm not sure how much.' The little dog cocked her head on one side intelligently, as though listening to every word. Hester smiled and tickled her under her ear. 'Of course I know he, well, fancies me. I'd have to be pretty dim not to

172

realise that. Sometimes I even think he's in love with me, but I'm not sure—Jack's a very together sort of person, isn't he?'

Suddenly Hester was struck by the absurdity of confiding in a dog and laughed at herself. She made herself some coffee and curled up in a corner of one of the living-room couches to drink it, a book open on her knee. She made no attempt to read it, and just sat, staring into the flames of the log fire. Life had altered since the night of the dinner party; taken on a new dimension. It was not so much that her feelings for her husband had changed, more that some veil had been swept away from her mind, allowing her to see how she had always felt for him, right from the very beginning. Not that she intended to let him know. In fact she fought tooth and nail to hide it, leaning so far the other way in her efforts to conceal this new self-knowledge she appeared cool and collected to the point of indifference in Jack's eyes, as well she knew. Except in bed. There was nothing she could do about that. There they came together with a lack of inhibition that sent the blood rushing to Hester's face even to think of it. What would happen when her bed failed to hold such overtly demonstrated attraction was a spectre that haunted Hester. To banish it she had decided to re-educate herself, to keep abreast with current affairs, and began to work her way through every line of the daily papers instead of keeping to the music and book reviews and the crosswords. She even took to reading the electronics journals delivered to the house, so that she could ask intelligent questions, and listen to the answers with some degree of understanding.

To her satisfaction John had already fallen into the habit of discussing his day with her over dinner, which she waited to share with him however late he arrived home. They also played chess some evenings, if only for a short time, and left the chessboard set up so that they could take up where they left off, a game sometimes taking a week to reach checkmate. Hester knew Jack enjoyed her company as much as she was stimulated by his. They had all the ingredients for a happy marriage, in fact, except one. Hester sighed. John had been away for five days, and she had missed him badly. The bed seemed huge and cold without him, the evenings endless after Jo had gone to bed. Not even his nightly telephone call had been much help. John's telephone manner leaned to the brief and concise rather than the affectionate and conversational, and left Hester restless and dissatisfied. Alicia had driven over one evening for dinner, and stayed the night, which had helped, but the week had dragged, nevertheless.

John was flying down on the shuttle from Edinburgh, and would be home by dinner time. Hester had made his favourite liver pâté, a duck was waiting to be popped into the oven, even her special orange sauce merely needed heating up. All she had to do was put on the new dress bought only yesterday, and just get her act together for when he arrived, try to curb the delight she now experienced at the sight of her husband's tall, elegant figure, the aloof face beneath the smooth fair hair affecting her the same way it had the very first time she had ever laid eyes on him in her study in Orchard Crescent, before she knew who he was. It had been the bitterest blow of her life to discover he was her unknown seducer. But she had even begun to accept that eventually, until she found out about Laura.

That, however, was all behind her. Since meeting Laura in the flesh at last Hester no longer felt the same animosity towards her. She knew very well John had been speaking the truth about his relationship with Laura, however much the woman in question would have wished it different. And now Hester's qualms seemed foolish. Laura had dined at Prospect only the week before. Jack had invited his young assistant, Bruce Harrison, as a fourth, and the evening had been surprisingly entertaining. Laura was a very witty and amusing guest, frankly envious of Hester, but as she said so without beating about the bush, Hester took no offence, as none was meant.

'I envy you your little girl, Hester.' Laura's tone had been sincere, her voice wistful as she peeped in at the sleeping Jo. 'Oliver and I just didn't seem to click that way—perhaps if we had ...' She shrugged her shoulders in the Bill Blass dress, then smiled at Hester philosophically as they went to the bedroom to make repairs. 'But then I'm his third stab at matrimony, darling—definitely not third time lucky.'

'You were once—more than friends with Jack, though,' said Hester, deciding not to beat about her own particular bush. Laura eyed her in surprise, then turned her attention to her expertly cut hair.

'But never on an exclusive basis, Hester. To be frank, I would have liked it like that, but once I applied for the job of assistant all that finished. John has a rule about never mixing business and pleasure. I knew it beforehand, but gambled on my own attractions proving too much for him to resist. They weren't. End of story.'

'But when you called in at Camilla's that day,' asked Hester curiously. 'What exactly did you have in mind?'

'Precisely what you suspected, darling. Only I really didn't know John had married you again, and only the day before. My timing was really off, wasn't it? I was bitchy, I suppose, from sheer shock.' Laura smiled apologetically. 'I do apologise, now I know you better.'

'If you go through with the divorce, do you want to work for Jack again?' Hester asked.

'I'll take care Oliver gives me great dollops of alimony, darling, I assure you—no more working for my living ...' She looked at Hester, an odd expression in her dark eyes. 'Why do you call him "Jack"? No one else does.'

Hester had smiled a secretive little smile.

'Just a pet name, Laura, that's all.'

Hester stirred and made up the fire, yawning a little,

then went over to the window and frowned. A thick fog obscured the view to within a few yards of the window. She frowned. It was likely to be tricky fetching Jo in this. Hester hated fog, and hated driving in it even more. The telephone rang and she ran to answer it, surprised to hear Jo's excited voice on the line.

'Mummy, it's me!'

'Hello, me.'

'No, it's Jo, silly!' There was much giggling against a background of children's voices. 'Fiona's mummy says can I sleep here?'

Hester was amazed, and highly delighted at Jo's request.

'Do you really want to, darling?'

'Oh yes please, Mummy—can I?'

'Why yes, Baby, if——'

'Goody, goody, Fiona's mummy wants to talk to you.'

A friendly, high-pitched voice took over.

'Mrs Ransome? Hello there, Annabel Ridley here. I thought it more sensible to keep Jo here than bring you out in this beastly weather. My husband is marooned somewhere in darkest Cumbria and my car sounded distinctly unwell on the way home from school, so the transport this end's a bit dodgy.'

'That's extremely kind of you—if you're sure it's no trouble,' said Hester.

'Lord no. The other children live within walking distance, so it's only Jo. We'd love to have her. Come and collect her in the morning, have a coffee with us.'

Hester felt a little glow as she put the 'phone down. Annabel Ridley sounded like Camilla—probably went to the same school—and seemed just as friendly. Before Hester could get to the kitchen the telephone rang again. She raced to the study.

'Hello?' she said breathlessly.

'Hester?' said John's voice. 'Are you all right?'

'Yes. Fine. Where are you?'

'Still in Scotland, and grounded I'm afraid. I'm hiring

a car and driving down.'

'But Jack, it's a real pea-souper here! Can't you wait until tomorrow?'

'Why? Are you so keen to spend another night alone?'

Hester took a deep breath.

'No. I just thought it might be a tricky journey.'

'Forecast says it's clearing. Don't wait up if I'm late.' He rang off without even saying goodbye, and Hester stared at the receiver in frustration before slamming it down.

'Come on, Scrap,' she called. 'Let's go for a little walk before it gets dark.' She shrugged on a quilted jacket and wandered down the sloping lawn, shivering a little in the eerie twilight, feeling thoroughly out of sorts. It was hardly possible to see a hand in front of her face already, so heaven knew what conditions were like on the motorway. Jack was an obstinate idiot to insist on travelling in weather conditions like this, worrying her to death. Hester whistled to Scrap and marched up to the house, slamming the kitchen door behind her pettishly, then she put the duck in the refrigerator, followed by the orange sauce. Not much point in cooking *that* today. Jack would just have to take pot luck when he finally arrived home.

Hester rang her mother and had a long chat with her, happy to find her gallivanting parent at home.

'I never know when I'm going to find you in these days, Mother.'

'Would you prefer me to stay at home knitting, Hester?' Alicia's gentle irony calmed her daughter down.

'No. I wouldn't. Sorry. I'm just spooked by sheer solitude and inactivity today, that's all.' Hester explained about Jo and John.

'How encouraging that Jo actually wanted to spend a night away from home,' commented Alicia. 'A sure sign she's getting over that nasty business.'

'Yes. I was very surprised when she asked.'

'And the fog is hardly John's fault,' added Alicia drily.

'No.' Hester let out a sigh. 'I just wish he'd stay put, that's all—not insist on driving through it.'

'It's probably much worse where you are, Hester, near the river. It may be much clearer on the main roads.'

'I hope you're right.'

'Do I detect a note of anxiety, Hester?'

There was silence for a moment.

'You know very well you do, Mother,' said Hester at last.

'Yes darling. I've always known very well. Don't you think it's time you let John know as well?'

Hester bit her knuckle anxiously.

'I would, but—but I don't know whether he's interested.'

Mrs Price snorted inelegantly.

'Don't be such an idiot, Hester.'

Hester kept herself busy for the rest of the evening. She tidied the kitchen drawers, peeled vegetables, made a cake, finished off two crosswords and tried to read. Her mind refused to stay on the book so she switched on the television and sat doggedly through two newscasts in case there was a report on traffic accidents, then went to have a bath. She gave herself a manicure and put on her new dress, then rang up Lucy and had a long chat to pass the time. Finally, almost ready to scream with anxiety, she took the dress off again and put on a nightgown and robe, made up the fire and poured herself a drink. There was an x-rated film on television, but watching the cavortings of naked bodies on the screen vaguely embarrassed her, and she turned it off in favour of the radio. Traffic reports gave news of general fog gradually clearing, with no mention of pile-ups on motorways, but by midnight Hester had reached a nadir of despair, certain something had happened to John.

When a car finally drew up outside the house just before one, Hester got up, trembling, waiting for the doorbell to ring, quite certain it was the police. The sound of a key in the door hardly registered, and she watched the front door opening, her feet glued in one spot, refusing to move. John came in, dumping down his hold-all, his face ashen and his eyes bloodshot with fatigue. Hester's instinct was to rush to him, smother him with kisses, hold him tightly in her arms and pour out her joy at having him home safely. Habit prompted her to say acidly,

'Were all the telephones out of order on the M6, Jack? A progress report would have been considerate.'

John stopped short, his face grim.

'I had a breakdown which took some time to get fixed. I tried to ring you twice. The line was engaged both times.'

Hester felt very small, all her anger draining away to leave her cold.

'Oh, I see. I'm sorry,' she said stiffly. 'Are you hungry? I'll get you something to eat.'

'Please don't bother.' John turned away wearily. 'I'll just have a shower and turn in.' He went downstairs without a backward glance and Hester looked after him in anguish. She felt like kicking herself, and drearily went round turning out lights and drawing back curtains. Ironically the fog had cleared and stars were shining in the sky. A bit late, she thought. For a good many things. As she left the living-room John came racing up the stairs.

'Where's Jo?' he demanded harshly.

Hester felt ashamed. She should have told him immediately he arrived.

'She's staying the night at Fiona's—the birthday party she was going to. I'm sorry, Jack—I should have told you at once.'

He slumped against the bannister and passed a hand wearily through his hair.

'It was a shock, seeing her bed empty—only Scrap in residence.'

'I know. Scrap considers it her rightful place.'

They looked at each other for a moment.

'I'm sorry,' said Hester diffidently. 'I shouldn't have ripped at you like that, but I was getting a bit anxious.'

John eyed her dispassionately.

'Why?'

'I thought you'd had an accident.'

'Would you have worried?'

'Of course! What do you think I'm made of?'

He shrugged.

'It's supposed to be sugar and spice, Hester, but sometimes its hard to believe.'

Her eyes fell.

'Yes, I suppose it is.' She cleared her throat. 'Why don't you have a hot bath and relax a bit, and I'll bring you some supper on a tray to the bedroom.'

'It might be better if I slept in the spare room tonight,' he said off-handedly.

Hester took a deep breath.

'All right,' she said levelly. 'I'll bring the tray there.'

'Fine.' John went downstairs and Hester slowly crossed the hall to the kitchen, fighting back tears. She made tea, toasted quantities of bread and wrapped it in a napkin, added her home-made pâté to the tray and took it downstairs to the spare room, but it was in darkness. She could hear John whistling in their own bathroom and went into the bedroom, setting the tray down on his bedside table.

'I'll sleep in the other room,' she called through the half open door. 'You stay here.'

'Don't be silly. You'll sleep here as usual. I was just being niggardly and retaliatory.'

'Oh.'

John came into the bedroom, rubbing at his wet hair with the sleeve of his robe. He examined the contents of the tray with satisfaction.

'Looks good, Hester, but I'd dearly love a whisky and soda for starters.'

'I'll fetch it.' She flew back upstairs and collected a glass, whisky bottle and soda syphon and returned to their room, where John was propped up against the headboard eating toast and pâté with enjoyment.

'Good paté,' he said, his mouth full. 'Yours?'

She nodded and poured him a drink. He drank it straight down, and gave a deep sigh.

'That's a lot better. Now tell me all this about Jo.'

Hester sat down on the edge of the bed, and told him about Jo's unexpected phone call, and Annabel Ridley's friendly little message.

'Jo was all for it, to my surprise. Do you think she's really over the kidnap at last, Jack?'

'If not completely over it Jo seems to have made a big step in the right direction—do you think I could have a little more toast?'

Hester had a suspicion John was enjoying watching her run about at his behest. Not that she minded—she owed him something for her pig of a greeting, if for nothing else. Eventually he polished off the best part of a loaf of bread and most of the pâté, plus two whiskies. Hester could only be persuaded to share his pot of tea.

'You've had dinner long ago, I suppose,' he said casually, and Hester avoided a direct answer by collecting the tray and taking it up to the kitchen. And having taken the time to wash cups and plates she found it needed a double dose of courage to go back down to the bedroom. John was finishing his third glass of whisky as she got back, which was unusual, as his taste for alcohol was usually more temperate.

'You must be tired,' he said. 'Come to bed.'

Obediently Hester took off her robe and switched off her bedside lamp, then slid carefully into her side of the bed. She lay flat and tried to relax, aware that John was watching her.

'Are you all prepared to lie there and think of

England?' he asked, and even with eyes tightly shut Hester could tell he was grinning. Without waiting for an answer he got up and went to the bathroom, where Hester could hear him cleaning his teeth, humming under his breath. His high spirits jarred on her and she turned on her side, towards the edge of the bed. A moment later the other light went out and John came in beside her.

'Good night, Hester,' he said pleasantly.

'Good night.' Hester stared into the darkness, doing her best to pretend she was alone in the bed. They had obviously reached a new turning point in their relationship. Up to now he would either have begun to make love to her at this stage, or cuddled her closely against him to sleep. Not tonight, apparently. All at once it was too much. Hot, stinging tears slid down Hester's cheeks, running down into her pillow, and she had to sniff. She turned face down to muffle her distress, then a kind, impersonal voice asked.

'Would you like a handkerchief?'

Mortified, she nodded, forgetting he couldn't see. John must have felt her movement and fished in his bedside table drawer in the dark, then put a handkerchief under her pillow. Hester snatched it and blew into it, not caring if the sound were comic, only conscious of a thick grey misery that enveloped her like the fog of earlier on. She pushed her hair away from her neck and turned her pillow over, wishing bitterly she had moved into the other room.

'What's the matter, Hester?' asked John softly. 'What's making you so unhappy?'

There seemed no point in telling him *he* was.

'Nothing—at least, nothing I can really explain,' she said indistinctly.

'Why not?' He waited for her to answer, but the words refused to come. With a sigh he reached for her and pulled her into his arms, which put paid to the last shreds of Hester's self-control. She cried her eyes out against his shoulder, all the strain and worry of the long wait dissolving into a cleansing flood that washed her clean of any feeling at all. For a long time after her tears had dried Hester lay still in John's arms. He held her close in silence, stroking her tangled curls, and eventually she drew away a little.

'I'm very sorry, Jack. You can expect to do this for Jo, but not for me.'

'The tears don't worry me, Hester. I'm more concerned with their cause.'

Hester felt too drained to dissemble further.

'I was worried to death about you, so of course, when you finally arrived I snapped your head off.' She felt his body tense and curved herself closer to him.

'Does that mean you do have some sort of feeling for me after all?' he asked.

'You know I do,' she muttered into his shoulder.

'I had hoped,' he said almost musingly. 'but I rather thought any feelings you had were physical more than anything else.'

Hester went hot.

'Am I so—so——'

'Responsive, darling.' He laughed softly, then stopped as a long tremor ran through her body. 'What's the matter? Cold?'

She shook her head silently, not ready to tell him that the word 'darling' had affected her like an electric shock.

'We have a certain physical rapport, wouldn't you agree?' he asked. 'Chemistry I suppose one calls it. Whatever it is happens the instant we touch, which explains my unprecedented behaviour that first night in Camilla's guest room. Explains but not excuses, I hasten to add. God knows it had never happened like that before. Dare I suppose the same thing happens for you, too, Hester?'

'Yes,' she said honestly.

'Have many other men made love to you since——'

'No.'

'Why not?' John's voice sounded strained.

'After the experience with you it, well——'

'Put you off men for life, I suppose!'

'I suppose you could put it like that.'

John laughed shortly.

'God, Hester, I'll never live it down, will I?'

Suddenly it was all so simple. Hester had no interest in hiding her feelings any longer. She knew John was fond of her, and she owed him the truth, one way and another. She wriggled away and sat up, switching on her lamp. With deliberation she stacked her pillows behind her and looked down into John's upturned face as he lay on his stomach, his head propped up on his hands, a watchful look in his eyes.

'You mistook my meaning, Jack,' she said simply. 'Other men, not you. Knowing you spoiled me for anyone else.'

He lay very still, his face a blank.

'Then would you mind telling me why you were so adamant about a divorce?' he asked carefully.

'Post-natal dementia, I think,' she informed him solemnly. 'I went into labour with Jo a bit early because I heard about your accident and learned about Laura more or less simultaneously. It was all a bit much. And no sooner was I over the birth than I saw that piece about you both in the Sunday papers. I was paranoid with jealousy. I persuaded myself you were enjoying the delights of Laura's bed while shackled to me out of sheer guilty conscience.'

John stared at her, his eyes for once completely unguarded.

'What?' He blinked and shook his head, as if clearing his brain.

'There's more,' said Hester, determined to get it all off her chest. 'The moment I saw you hanging over Jo's cot I hit on the most effective form of retaliation possible.'

'You certainly did!' His eyes narrowed. 'Why were you so vindictive?'

She looked away.

'You told me once that if we'd met under ordinary circumstances, in practically any other way, you'd have done your best to get to know me, ask me out to dinner——'

'What I really meant, Hester, was that one look at you was all it took for me to know I'd found exactly what I'd been subconsciously looking for all my life.'

She looked back at him quickly, then nodded, reassured by the naked truth in his eyes.

'It was the same for me too.'

John lay flat abruptly, his head buried in the pillow.

'Are you all right?' she demanded.

He sat up again, glaring at her, his eyes glittering with rage.

'No, I am not all right,' he said acidly. 'This moment of instant recognition, this feeling you had; presumably it died the moment you learned my identity!'

Hester backed away a little.

'No. I just felt a terrible anger and disappointment. The—the rest remained unchanged. Why else do you suppose I married you. The first time, I mean.'

'You tell me!' he said savagely. 'I always assumed it was to acquire a wedding ring. You made it crystal clear you had no use for a husband.'

'Only in the beginning, Jack. After a time I began to look forward to your visits enormously to allow my initial feeling to take over. I had only been so bitter because you felt *obliged* to marry me, you see.'

'No I don't see. I wanted to marry you, dammit.' John scowled at her, and pushed a hand through his hair.

'Well I didn't know that, did I?' Hester was beginning to regret her urge to confess. She had dimly pictured a pretty scene where John swept her into his arms and they lived happily ever after, but it was turning out quite differently. He seemed to be getting more furious with her by the minute.

'All I know is that we've wasted five bloody stupid years of separation, Hester. I told you as bluntly as possible that after meeting you I led a totally celibate life. I explained that Laura was just a business associate. What else was I suppose to say, or do?'

They stared at each other in hostile silence, John's eyes wintry with anger, Hester's jewel-green with resentment. Then the ice in John's eyes melted, the rigid expression of his face softened, and involuntarily Hester put out a hand towards him. He caught it in his and carried it to his mouth, his eyes still holding hers.

'Well, Hester,' he said softly, with the caressing note that always turned her bones to water. 'Why did you marry me?'

Her tear-damp lashes swept down to veil her eyes.

'Because I wanted to, I suppose.'

He inched his way closer.

'And why did you want to?'

'Because I loved you.' She let out a shaky breath. There. It was out at last.

John was not satisfied.

'Loved?' he persisted.

'Why do I have to do all the confessing?' she asked, her eyes suddenly opening wide. 'You never say you love *me*, not even when, when——'

'I make love to you?' he suggested. 'But I don't just love you in bed, sweetheart, I love you when you're cooking, when you're covered with mud grubbing about in the garden, when you bite the tip of your tongue over your interminable crosswords, and particularly when you wear that desperate frown of concentration on the other side of the chessboard.' He paused, smiling, as her eyes filled with disbelief, the colour flooding from the edge of her nightgown to the roots of her hair. 'I could just have paid you maintenance that first time, you know,' he went on prosaically. 'I needn't have married you to support you both. I married you, Hester, because I wanted to, both times. I must admit that Jo being kidnapped was hardly the way I would have chosen to bring us together again. But now that she seems fully recovered from the experience I can't say I feel quite so hostile to the "Saviours of the Earth" as I should.'

'Jack, really!' she remonstrated, smiling at him in mock reproval.

'Make no mistake,' he said, his face hardening. 'If I'd laid hands on either of that happy pair for weeks after they took Jo I wouldn't have been responsible for the consequences. Tonight I feel different, that's all.'

'Yes, so do I.'

John leaned an arm against the headboard, his face almost touching hers.

'When are we expected to pick up Jo?'

Hester stared dreamily up into his eyes.

'For coffee, Mrs Ridley said.'

'I expect they have coffee fairly late, wouldn't you say?' He looked at his watch, then dropped a kiss on the tip of her nose. 'Which means we have roughly seven hours before we need stir out of this bed.'

Hester reached out a hand and turned off the light, then slid her arms round his neck, muttering indistinctly into his chest, as his arms closed tightly, locking her against him. He nudged the curls away from her ear with his lips.

'Did you say "bliss" or "kiss"?' he whispered.

Hester turned her mouth up to meet his, stretching luxuriously.

'Either one, Jack. They mean pretty much the same thing.'

Coming Next Month in Harlequin Presents!

863 MATCHING PAIR Jayne Bauling
A lounge singer and a hotel owner are two of a kind. He chooses to live life on the surface; she feels she has no choice. Neither have been touched by love.

864 SONG OF A WREN Emma Darcy
Her friend and lodger, a terrible tease, introduces her to his family in Sydney as his "live-in lady." No wonder his brother deliberately downplays their immediate attraction.

865 A MAN WORTH KNOWING Alison Fraser
A man worth knowing, indeed! An English secretary decides that an American author is not worth getting involved with...as if the choice is hers to make.

866 DAUGHTER OF THE SEA Emma Goldrick
A woman found washed ashore on a French Polynesian island feigns amnesia. Imagine her shock when her rescuer insists that she's his wife, the mother of his little girl!

867 ROSES, ALWAYS ROSES Claudia Jameson
Roses aren't welcome from the businessman a London *pâtisserie* owner blames for her father's ruin. She rejects his company, but most of all she rejects his assumption that her future belongs with him.

868 PERMISSION TO LOVE Penny Jordan
Just when a young woman resigns herself to a passionless marriage to satisfy her father's will, the man in charge of her fortune and her fate withholds his approval.

869 PALE ORCHID Anne Mather
When a relative of his wrongs her sister, a secretary confronts the Hawaiian millionaire who once played her for a fool. She expects him to be obstructive—not determined to win her back.

870 A STRANGER'S TOUCH Sophie Weston
One-night stands are not her style. Yet a young woman cannot deny being deeply touched by the journalist who stops by her English village to recover from one of his overseas assignments.

WORLDWIDE LIBRARY IS YOUR TICKET TO ROMANCE, ADVENTURE AND EXCITEMENT

Experience it all in these big, bold Bestsellers— Yours exclusively from WORLDWIDE LIBRARY WHILE QUANTITIES LAST

To receive these Bestsellers, complete the order form, detach and send together with your check or money order (include 75¢ postage and handling), payable to WORLDWIDE LIBRARY, to:

In the U.S.
WORLDWIDE LIBRARY
Box 52040
Phoenix, AZ
85072-2040

In Canada
WORLDWIDE LIBRARY
P.O. Box 2800, 5170 Yonge Street
Postal Station A, Willowdale, Ontario
M2N 6J3

Quant.	Title	Price
_____	**WILD CONCERTO**, Anne Mather	$2.95
_____	**A VIOLATION**, Charlotte Lamb	$3.50
_____	**SECRETS**, Sheila Holland	$3.50
_____	**SWEET MEMORIES**, LaVyrle Spencer	$3.50
_____	**FLORA**, Anne Weale	$3.50
_____	**SUMMER'S AWAKENING**, Anne Weale	$3.50
_____	**FINGER PRINTS**, Barbara Delinsky	$3.50
_____	**DREAMWEAVER**, Felicia Gallant/Rebecca Flanders	$3.50
_____	**EYE OF THE STORM**, Maura Seger	$3.50
_____	**HIDDEN IN THE FLAME**, Anne Mather	$3.50
_____	**ECHO OF THUNDER**, Maura Seger	$3.95
_____	**DREAM OF DARKNESS**, Jocelyn Haley	$3.95

	YOUR ORDER TOTAL	$_____
	New York and Arizona residents add appropriate sales tax	$_____
	Postage and Handling	$ .75
	I enclose	$_____

NAME _____

ADDRESS _____ APT.# _____

CITY _____

STATE/PROV. _____ ZIP/POSTAL CODE _____

WW3

What the press says about Harlequin romance fiction...

"When it comes to romantic novels...
Harlequin is the indisputable king."
— *New York Times*

"...always with an upbeat, happy ending."
— *San Francisco Chronicle*

"Women have come to trust these
stories about contemporary people,
set in exciting foreign places."
— *Best Sellers*, New York

"The most popular reading matter of
American women today."
— *Detroit News*

"...a work of art."
— *Globe & Mail*, Toronto

Can you keep a secret?

You can keep this one plus 4 free novels